NOWHERE AGAIN!

NOWHERE AGAIN!

Jenny Sullivan

PONT BOOKS

First Impression – 2004

ISBN 1 84323 297 9

© Jenny Sullivan

Jenny Sullivan has asserted her right
under the Copyright, Designs and Patents Act, 1988,
to be identified as Author of this Work.

This book is published with the financial support of the
Welsh Books Council.

Printed in Wales at
Gomer Press, Llandysul, Ceredigion, Wales.

This book is dedicated
to the memory of my dear father-in-law
Bill Sullivan 1920-2003

THE MAKING OF THE SEA-HARP

Once, in the land of long-ago, when the earth was different but people were not, there was a boy. His name was Owain.

Owain was a musician, for the first sound that he heard as he lay on his mother's heart on the night that he was born was the incomparable song of a nightingale. Owain heard the thrilling, liquid sound, and ever after, music became his life. It whirled in his bones and his blood, and Owain became a Bard. He sang for Myrddin ap Emrys, whom you may know as Merlin; for Arthur and his Queen, Gwenhwyfar; for crowned heads and peasant folk, and when he sang even the birds listened.

Owain was in love with Sound. Blessed with purest pitch, he could imitate the notes of a lark, a blackbird or the rippling wind, and his voice enchanted all who heard it.

But Owain was always seeking new sounds, new voices to add to his own: never satisfied, he travelled to the Out Isles and to the land that Madoc of Wales discovered. He visited the snowy wastes of the Norselands and learned to imitate the deep notes of the gyrfalcon, and to the Mediterranean for the tinkling song of the tiny yellow Serin finch. All these and more he Heard and Knew, and Sang. He could imitate the howl of a wolf, the deep cough of a lion, even the brittle, light-filled music of the stars, but – he could not sing the sound of the sea. The sea had so many voices. It whispered the lapping of tiny rivulets on a sandy shore; it roared the mighty blast of a gale-driven ocean; it was the crash and splatter of foam on rock. The sea was always changing – the note, the pitch, the song, always different. Whenever the Bard imagined he knew it, the sea changed its song. It became Owain's dream and his nightmare; it haunted him.

Merlin might help. Merlin knew everything, even then, though he was in his youth and strength, and a long way from the old and bearded magician of legend. He spent his days in a Tower in the High King's castle, experimenting with weird ingredients, magical incantations and mysterious machines. Owain sought him out.

'Tell me the secret of the sea,' he begged. 'I will sing for you always, if you will tell me.'

Merlin adjusted a small cog and pulled a great lever. 'The secret of the sea?' he muttered absent-mindedly. 'No one knows the secret of the sea.'

'No one?'

'No one – except the Sea King, of course.'

'Then I shall ask the Sea King. Where shall I find him?'

Merlin peered at Owain over his spectacles. 'Where do you think? At the bottom of the sea, Bard!'

Owain took a boat onto the great expanse of the ocean. The Island of the Mighty receded, and soon he was alone on the Middlesome Sea. No land was visible, just the vast, heaving, singing waters. Owain

7

opened his throat and sang the sea's song, or tried to, but as the first notes issued forth, the sea's song changed, and Owain's song was spoiled.

'Sea King!' he shouted, cupping his hands about his mouth. 'Sea King, I want to talk to you. Listen to me, Sea King!'

The Sea King heard, but the Sea King was not to be summoned by a mortal. He grew angry, and sent a surge of water beneath Owain's little boat. The boat tossed and spun, until Owain was mightily sea-sick, and then, when Owain was as miserable as it is possible for a human to be and still survive, the Sea King overturned the boat.

Owain was tipped out. He sank and sank through the green depths, down and down, escorted by mackerel and seals, dolphin and porpoise, until his quivering toes touched sun-dappled sand.

The Sea King, his mighty iridescent tail curled about him, his head wreathed in a halo of silvery fish, folded his arms and scowled at the Bard.

'Who disturbs the Sea King?' he thundered, with the voice of a wild sea on a stormy night.

'It is I, Owain the Bard,' Owain replied, marvelling that he could breathe so far beneath the waves.

'What do you want, Owain the Bard?' the Sea King bellowed, with the voice of a swelling tide pounding a rudderless ship.

'I want to sing the sound of the sea,' Owain replied. 'I can sing all the sounds of the world, but the voice of the sea eludes me.'

'Of course it does!' the Sea King roared, with the

voice of a tidal wave swooping on a defenceless shore. 'The sea does not have a single voice! The sea is all voices, all sounds. How can you, a mere mortal, expect to sing them all?'

'You could teach me,' Owain pleaded. 'If you please, your Highness!'

'And what will you give me if I do?' the Sea King whispered, with the sound of the incoming tide creeping over ridged sand. 'What?'

Owain thought for a while. What could he offer? He had riches, he was well paid for his songs, but the Sea King would surely scorn mere gold. And then he had an idea. 'If,' he said at last, 'you will teach me to sing like the sea, then I will make you a musical instrument that will sing like the rain. In the sea, you have never heard the rain when it falls on a leaf, on dry earth, on a slate roof. I will bring the music of the rain to you.'

'The rain, eh?' the Sea King mused, in a voice like the sea lapping at the sides of a rowboat. 'I've never heard the rain. Very well, Owain the Bard, if within the turn of seven tides you bring me the sound of the rain, then I shall teach you to sing like the sea.'

Owain bowed, and swam away, escorted by the Sea King's daughter, a beautiful mermaid, who was fascinated by this strange, tail-less creature.

'Owain,' she sang, in the voice of the sea lapping shells, 'let me help you, Owain the Bard.'

'Find me a shell,' Owain commanded, 'a pure white shell as large as my head. The inside must be smooth and pink as silk, and the outside unblemished.

9

'And what will you give me, Owain the Bard?' the mermaid asked, in a voice like seawater caressing a fish.

'I will give you – gold?' Owain suggested.

'Gold?' the mermaid mocked, in a voice like the sea drifting through the ragged sides of a sunken boat. 'I have all the treasures of the ocean!'

'Then what do you want?' Owain asked.

'I want you!' the mermaid replied, her voice so soft that it was like the stillest of tides at night. 'I want you, Owain the Bard, for my husband!'

'Agreed!' Owain said, although he had no intention of marrying a fish-woman.

Happy with her bargain, the Sea King's Daughter swam away, and soon returned with a perfect shell as large as Owain's head, and as pink, silky and smooth inside as Owain could wish.

'When you come back, Owain the Bard,' she whispered, her voice like crisp foam bursting on sand, 'we shall be together, you promise?'

'I promise,' Owain replied, and kicking out with his feet, returned to the surface, where his boat, righted and emptied, awaited him.

While the tide ebbed and swelled, ebbed and swelled, Owain worked on the sea shell. First he bored tiny holes in the outer rim of the open mouth, smoothing and polishing as he went, so that no rough edges would sharpen the tone. Then he made harp-strings of purest silver, mined from the Northern hills, and threaded them through the holes, drawing them through and fastening them. Finally, he tuned the *shell, tightening and loosening the strings until the sound that came from the empty shell was exactly the sound of soft rain, falling. Falling on leaves, on water, on earth, on stone, on slate.*

Then, when the tide had turned seven times, Owain returned to the Sea King's domain.

The Sea King was enchanted with Owain's work. He played the Sea Harp over and over, delighting in the tinkling, pattering, miraculous sounds. In return, as he had promised, he taught Owain how to sing the sound of the sea in all its moods. At last, Sea King and Bard parted, and Owain made to go.

But he had forgotten his promise: the love-lorn mermaid followed him, pleading with him to stay.

'You promised,' she cried, in a voice like sea-water trickling between stones.

'What do I want with a woman with a tail?' Owain cried, imitating her voice perfectly.

'But you promised,' she said again, weeping, her voice the sound of seawater moaning in a cave.

'And I break my promise!' Owain said, his voice grumbling like a rising tide. 'Go away, fish-woman!'

He reached his boat and clambered in, water streaming from his clothes. Triumphantly he opened his throat and sang like the sea.

The mermaid swam round the little boat, weeping bitterly. Owain reached for his oars and, still singing, began to row. In a fury, the Sea King's Daughter caught the side of the boat and pulled. Green water flooded into the little vessel until it filled and sank, and Owain the Bard who could sing like the sea, floundered in the water. He sank ever deeper, but this time he could not breathe . . .

The mermaid watched as the drowning Bard sank down through the sunlit sea, his beautiful voice silenced for ever.

And that, my friends, is how the Sea Harp came to be made.

THE SKY EGG STORY

You do not believe in dragons? I can tell you that there were and will be dragons: why else would the whole world tell tales of them in the firelight? I am sure that you have no difficulty in believing in dinosaurs; after all, there are museums in which you an admire their whitened bones. But what is a dinosaur, if it is not a great lizard-like creature with fanged jaws and sharp talons – in short, a dragon. Some dragons flew, some walked, and for certain their breath was so hot it could be mistaken for flame. Besides, I know there are dragons. I know . . .

Of course I know. Yet, once upon a rainbow, when knights rode the Island of the Mighty, righting wrongs and pursuing Quests, dragons were already walking the road to extinction. Humans were reluctant to share their living space with large scaly creatures with an unfortunate taste for human flesh. And so the dragons were hunted and killed, before they even left the nest. How brave, to kill a small, blind creature scarce able to crawl! But dragons were hated, and soon, because of relentless killing, there was only one dragon left in the whole wild wondrous world.

Not every one in the world hated dragons: there was a small girl, no one important, no one of whom you might have heard, whose name was Siwan.

Her family was poor and powerless and Siwan, although she was barely twelve, worked hard, as everyone poor did in those days. Siwan's tasks were many: sowing and reaping in season, fetching water from the stream and gathering sticks to keep the fire burning. Fire was heat and light, and animals feared it, and fire was essential. Siwan was gathering twigs and branches when she first met her dragon.

You probably will not believe me when I tell you that child and beast became friends: but for all that, it is true. The dragon was large, and by rights should have been slaughtered with the rest of its kind. But this dragon was able to hide in a cave big enough to conceal it entirely, and only Siwan knew where it hid. It may surprise you to learn that dragons are gentle creatures, especially the females, and more especially when they are breeding, although naturally they are protective of their young. The last male dragon had long since been slaughtered, but dragons lay eggs, of course, and strangely, can choose a safe time for the birth of their young.

The she-dragon knew that now was not a good time to lay her eggs: only by chance had she escaped death when her mate had been hunted and killed, and before she laid them, she needed to find a place where her babies could be born. At last, she found it, her secret cave, and here she believed that her babies would be safe.

But sadly, even the best-kept secrets sometimes escape. Siwan's uncle noticed that the girl often disappeared for long periods of time, and often returned empty-handed when she should have been laden with firewood. So, curious, he followed her one day, and saw her enter a cave, high in the mountains. He waited until she emerged, and then crept into the cave to see where she had been and what she had been doing. He was an unpleasant man, who took pleasure in telling tales on Siwan, and seeing her beaten.

He went silently, silently, and it is as well that he did, for if the dragon had heard him, she would have killed him to keep her secret and protect her young. As well for him, that is. But not for the dragon, who had laid the last clutch of dragon eggs in the whole world.

The eggs were beautiful; blue as all the blues in the universe, their surface shifting and changing like oil in a puddle. Sky, aquamarine, turquoise, gentian, bluebell, forget-me-not, moonlight-on-snow, think of an infinite blueness, and imagine it there, swirling on the surface of the dragon eggs.

Siwan's uncle could not see the eggs, for the great beast was shielding them with her body, but as soon as he saw the dragon he slithered out of the cave, and ran as fast as he could back to the village. He gathered a band of men with spears and axes and swords and together they climbed the mountain to kill the last dragon in the world.

Siwan saw them go, and knew that she must try to save her friend. Her heart breaking, she climbed the mountain another way, and reached the cave a little before the killers.

'Fly away, dragon!' she screamed, 'they are coming to kill you!'

The creature bent her head sorrowfully, knowing

that if she flew, she would have to abandon her precious eggs, and then the Dragonfolk would be finished forever. But if she stayed, then the approaching death-dealers would destroy her and her eggs, too. They had discovered her secret cave, and all was lost. All the same, the she-dragon would not leave her unhatched babies.

Siwan pushed and shoved at the dragon, but her tiny strength was useless. But then the dragon did a strange thing: she bent her head and nudged one of the eggs from beneath her body. It rolled from under her, rolled and rolled until it came to rest at Siwan's feet. Siwan looked from the egg to the dragon and back again, and understood. She picked it up and thrust it inside her tunic.

The egg was ice cold, for dragons are cold-blooded creatures, and their eggs are not hatched by warmth. A dragon-egg taken from the nest will gradually warm to human blood-heat, but as soon as it is replaced beneath a mother-dragon, her body temperature chills it. Just before it hatches, the egg becomes hotter and hotter as the tiny creature inside uses its fiery breath to crack the hard shell.

The dragon nudged the child again, and she staggered, and then, as the sound of men's voices came closer, Siwan ran. Clutching the precious egg she flew, blinded by tears, frantically searching for a place to hide her precious burden. Dreadful roars and screams of pain came from the cave: the dragon was dying, and her remaining eggs were stamped underfoot.

There was nowhere Siwan could hide the egg. Sooner or later the men would find it and all would be lost. The icy egg chilled her body, and she shivered. And then she thought: there was one place that was cold as cold, where no one would ever find it, where perhaps, just perhaps, it might survive and one day hatch. It was a terrible chance, but it was all there was.

Siwan ran until she reached the magical place where the mountains were reflected in the sea. Standing on the smooth sand, she took the egg from under her tunic, kissed it, and threw it with all her might. It barely splashed, and the last, precious dragon egg in the world sank, sank, sank down to the Kingdom of the Sea.

One day, perhaps, the blue egg, blue as the sky, blue as blueness itself, will be found, perhaps dredged to the surface by a fisherman's net, perhaps cast ashore by a mighty sea. Who can say? Not I, certainly, for with dragons all things are possible.

Of course there were dragons. And one day there may be a dragon again.

THE EARTHSTONE WITCH

Once, there was a Witch. We shall call her Gwawr. That is not her name, but her name, you see, is an Old Name, and it is better not to speak an Old Name aloud.

Gwawr lived a long, long time ago. She had seen the great dragons come and go; the coming and melting of the ice; the taming of fire; men of stone; men of iron, and still Gwawr lived. She lived to see the land that had once been volcanic rock and vast sheets of ice grow green and become beautiful.

She lived so long that her beautiful land began to change once more. Man discovered that fire could change earth's ores into metal. That was the beginning of the destruction, and as Time slowly passed, Gwawr's precious land became covered in ugly chimneys vomiting smoke, giant factories sprawling across green-ness, and metal machines running on rails and roads across her domain.

Gwawr, at last, grew angry. She decided that she would make a spell so powerful that it would either return the world to its former beauty, or destroy it altogether. Such a spell is not easy, and is beyond perilous to its maker. It takes months and years of work to devise it, centuries to collect the ingredients for the mixture, and aeons to produce the magical potion but, undaunted, Gwawr set to work. She had nothing, any more, but Time.

She collected dragons' tears glimmering in the setting sun; the long-drawn patterns of the moon on water; the horny toenail of the last living giant. She plunged deep beneath the sea to steal a lock of a mermaid's hair. Still she did not have all that the spell required.

She dug deep in the earth to find the first stone tool ever made by man – a clumsy hammerhead; she tunnelled into mountains to find gold, silver and diamonds; she added the sound of water pouring down the slopes of Eryri, and mixed in the first drop of rain that fell on All Hallows Eve.

She sprinkled in earth from a magician's grave, a feather from the Owl that was Blodeuwedd, and a splinter of the True Cross, for she believed in the Good Magic even though she was a witch.

At last everything was ready; Gwawr put all she had collected into a cauldron made of star-metal that had fallen from the skies on Midsummer's Day, added seven crystalline unicorn tears and the eyelash of a hippogriff, and began to stir. When a year had passed she added eleven tablespoonfuls of snowmelt from the purest part of the Northern Icefields, and stirred again for seven-times-seven years and three hours, seven and three being All-Powerful Numbers.

The potion diminished to a mere cupful. Gwawr put it in a pot of purest silver and heated it until the cupful was reduced to a spoonful of greyish-brown powder.

Emptying the powder carefully into a golden goblet, Gwawr added the final ingredient. I shall not *tell you what it was, for if you should try to replicate the spell, it would be dangerous for you. All that I will say is that it was liquid . . .*

Gwawr stirred the mixture, and when liquid and powder were combined, she shut her eyes, and wished.

She wished for the land to be green again. For the skies to be pure and clear, so that stars could be seen in all their beauty. For trees and flowers, birds and beasts, all to live in safety. For the rivers and seas to be crystal clean as once they had been, and for all the terrible machines that men had made for manufacture, motion and warfare, to vanish in a mighty puff of smoke.

And then, Gwawr drank the potion.

It scalded her as she drank, although it was not hot. The potion was so powerful that even the Witch's magical body could not endure it. The potion slid down Gwawr's throat, through her gullet – and into her stomach. Gwawr, you see, was old and becoming forgetful, and had failed to protect herself by drinking the Milk of Human Kindness before she swallowed the potion.

Gwawr died instantly, but the magic of the potion had already flooded into her bloodstream, pumped into her heart – and turned it to pure crystal in a moment of white hot fusion. The rest of her body was changed by incredible heat, enclosing the crystal in an oval of heavy earthstone. All the magic that had been in the potion was concentrated now in a dull-looking, heavy stone with a crystal heart. The Earthstone.

All that was left of Gwawr the Witch lay lost in the grass of a summer meadow until one afternoon a small boy discovered it. His name does not matter: he has only a small part to play. He picked up the Earthstone and brushed the mud from its surface. The pure crystal sparkled. The boy, as boys will, tried to tear the shining crystal heart from the ugly stone, but could not shift it. So the boy took his treasure home, carried carefully between the palms of his hands, to show his father in their house beside the sea.

But as soon as he placed the stone on the wooden table in the kitchen, a strange thing happened: the table shuddered, twitched – and roots grew from its legs, twisted through the floor. It put up a slender trunk, sprouted branches and leaves, and burst through the ceiling into the bedrooms. The Earthstone fell to the floor, and fell and fell, through carpet, floor and foundations, until it landed in the earth beneath the house which no man's hand had ever touched.

The father retrieved the stone, turned it over in his hands and wondered what use he could make of this magical thing. He experimented, and learned that whatever the hand of man had made or touched, the Earthstone returned it to its former state. Leather shoes became cows, woolly jumpers became sheep. Perhaps he could make money showing this thing to other people. He would be famous!

But the man did not understand magic. He was used to modern wonders: television, telephones. He *did not understand that magic is constantly working; that it cannot be switched on and off like an electric light. He did not understand that the only materials that could contain the Earthstone were either his own hands – or the finest iron box ever made, for magic, of course, is neutralised by iron. If Gwawr had lived, she could have told him: but if Gwawr had lived, who can say what might have happened?*

The Earthstone began to be troublesome. How could the man travel when he could not put the stone down? It turned his car to metal ore, a rubber tree and a heap of sand. It wrecked the furniture in his house, destroyed his clothes. His wife left him, because the man could not afford to keep replacing things the Earthstone had touched and destroyed, and she wanted her home as it had been. Bit by bit, everything the man treasured changed or disappeared, until one day, in desperation, he took the magic thing to the edge of the cliff near his home and threw it as far out to sea as he could. It soared through the air, and landed with a mighty splash.

And down it sank to the Kingdom of the Sea King, where – for a time at least – it was safe.

CHAPTER ONE

'*Bonjour*, Madame,' I said. '*Comment ça va?*'

Madame raised her eyebrows kind of French-ly. 'Youer accsont, Catreen Cherie, est trés terreeble!'

And yours ain't too hot, either Madame, I thought but didn't say. 'Hey, that's why I'm here, right Madame?'

Madame shrugged. 'We shell pairsevee-eur, *mais non?*'

'Yeah, sure, Madame. Let's persevere.'

Which was just what I didn't feel like doing. What I really wanted to do was anything else, like a couple of hundred miles away, right? But my Mom and Dad had decided that since I was in Europe anyhow, they might as well give me this like, huge advantage by sending me to France to learn French. Except I didn't wanna be in La Rochelle, France, staying *en famille* with Monsieur et Madame and their revolting daughter. I wanted to be home in Wales, close to Twm and all the things that kind of kept me breathing, you know? But hey. Only another two months and I could go back to Wales. Boy, was I looking forward to *that.*

When Madame turned me loose it was lunch time, and you know the French and lunch time. These guys never heard of fast food. It was a two-hour Event, three courses plus *café*. So it wasn't until nearly three o'clock that I managed to sneak off down to the harbour.

One thing about La Rochelle: there's a shipload of history there, and loads of stuff to look at, and this real great harbour full of little yachts and two huge towers, as well as a town with covered sidewalks so even if it rains you can still mooch in the dry. But today wasn't raining, it was glorious sunshine, which was why I'd resented the French lesson so much. I'd been there four months, starting in January, and it had been a long, wet, cold winter. Thank goodness I had the sea nearby. If Mom and Dad had sent me some place inland, I'd probably have like pined away and died by now.

I strolled out along the harbour, past the marina with its little, bobbing boats tethered to floating wooden boardwalks, between the two massive old chain-towers right to the very end of the man-made quays so I could look out across the sea. The sun was warm on my back and it reminded me of home – well, not home, which I guess is Pittsburgh, Pennsylvania, if I'm real picky – but of Wales, which is my second home and feels like it should be my first. I couldn't see Wales from there, OK, I know it. But it was the same sea stretching between La Rochelle and Wales, yeah? Kinda.

Although La Rochelle is real busy, even in April, I found myself alone on the end of the jetty. Clouds scudded across the sky, and there were little splashy-type wavelets white on the aquamarine sea. I just sat and kind of *gazed* for a bit, sitting on the edge, my legs dangling. Weed waved from the underwater walls, and small crabs scuttled, visible through the

24

clear water. Something caught my attention, a little way out.

Something long and sleek curved from the sea and sank again. I thought it was a trick of the light at first, but then it happened again. I shaded my eyes and watched the spot. There it was again, a sleek silver fin rose and rolled, sank again out of sight. And then, as if now it was certain it had my attention, a dolphin launched itself out of the water, droplets catching diamond light, arched gracefully and plunged back in. I glanced around to see if anyone else was watching, had seen, but there was no one near, no one looking. It was my private performance, and it wasn't over yet.

The dolphin came closer, closer, still unseen by anyone but me, until it was a grey shadow knifing through the clear water, so close that if the harbour wall hadn't been so high, I could have reached down and touched it. It circled and then rose, directly beneath me. The bulbous head and pointed nose cleared out of the water and a pair of intelligent eyes surveyed me knowingly. It bobbed and squeaked, then sank again – and was gone, as if it had never been there at all.

I was so thrilled it felt like my birthday. But still I didn't catch on that it wasn't just a coincidental sighting.

Back at the townhouse in *Rue Quatorze Juillet,* my Nemesis was waiting. Marie-Claire, Madame's daughter. She was such a total, utter dork, you know? I don't, like, hate her or anything, but we don't have one single thing in common. I tried real hard to find something, anything, honest I did, but there was just nothing except we were both female. Sometimes it was kind of hard, when she was rabbiting on about all these guys that are, like, *chasing* her and coming on to her. I'm just not interested in that stuff. I have Twm back home and I don't care to see any other guys – especially French guys, who all seem to think they're God's gift to girls because they're French, like we should be real grateful for that. I mean, duh!

Naturally Marie-Claire speaks almost perfect English with a real cute accent, but then, she's been learning it since she was a little kid, and I've only just had French inflicted on me. Mom's idea. Sure, I'll appreciate it when I'm real old and wanna get a job in the Euro-Parliament or something, but hey, I'm, like, sixteen, yeah? I don't want to even think about work yet. What I really want to do is go to school with Twm in Pontpentre-dŵr, not *école* in La Rochelle. But that's not gonna happen for another two months, when the semester back home will be almost done. Still, there'll be the summer to look forward to – unless Mom decides I need to learn German or Japanese next! But once I'm home I'm gonna refuse to go anyplace else, ever.

Meantime, there was Marie-Claire. 'Where have you been?' She was hanging over the balcony rail as I came up the garden path. 'I want to try on closes wiz you.'

'Out for a walk.' I mean, *try on clothes?* What planet was she from? 'Sorry. Didn't know you wanted a girlie afternoon.'

'*Mais*, Catrrreen, you know zat I like to spend time wiz you. You air my friend, and we 'ave only two monses left togezzer. Come upstairs quickly, Catrreen. I 'ave a new dress zat you mus' try on *immediatement.*'

'Yeah, sure,' I said, and plodded unhappily upstairs to her room. Which was pink and white and girly and frilly, just like Marie-Claire. The dress was definitely Marie-Claire getting sophisticated – short and sleek and black and plunging, but most definitely not me. I'm a Levis and t-shirt kind of girl, and I'd get so embarrassed if I went about showing my chests the whole time like she does. Mind, she's got chests to show, so that helps some, I guess. But all the same I had to try the darn thing on, pretend I liked it, let Marie-Claire fiddle with my hair (not a whole lot she can do to that: I had it cut majorly short three weeks ago in self-defence. But she still wants to put little sparkly bows and stuff in it. Like, no way! Sparkly bows? Sharp sticks and poked eyes, yeah?)

Then I had to shower and change for dinner, and make conversation – *en Français, cherie!* – which is real hard to do when a person is trying to concentrate on eating. Then I had to make like I was interested when *Monsieur* insisted on telling me everything that was in *France Jour* and *Paris Match* in his English, which is even worse than my French. So it was close to eleven o'clock before I got up to my room again, the only place I can get any peace, and not even there if Marie-Claire wants to tell me all about her love life with Jean-Daniel who, believe me, is a major, world-class nerd.

As soon as I got into my bedroom, I knew there was something different. I stood in the middle, beside my (frilly-curtained and valanced mock four-post) bed and turned, slowly, trying to work out what it was.

Nothing seemed out of place. My clothes were all neatly filed in my closet (which would really have amazed my Mom). The book I was reading was on he bedside table, my *"Llewelyn the Last Prince of Wales"* leather bookmark sticking out of it. My bathrobe hung on the back of the door, my bits of makeup and cleansers and stuff were all tucked in the drawer of the highboy. So, what?

Then I realised. It wasn't something I could *see*. It was something I could feel.

A vision of the dolphin flashed into my mind and as quickly disappeared. Perhaps the great creature visiting me hadn't just been coincidence. Had it been trying to tell me something, to communicate?

A feeling of anxiety slithered over me, like a goose walking on my grave. Then I realised why. The air in the room was *cold*. In a centrally heated house, on a warm April night, I could see my breath misting on the air. Now that was majorly weird.

I walked around the room hugging myself for warmth, trying to pick up what it was. It wasn't until I came close to the highboy that I realised that the cold was coming from there.

From the top drawer, to be exact. The drawer where, hidden beneath the elegant silk scarf that Marie-Claire had insisted on giving me, I had hidden my greatest treasure.

It was something Marie-Claire had never seen, *would* never see. Something more beautiful than the silk scarf, more beautiful than anything Marie-Claire could even imagine. Something that would probably look, to her, like a painted pebble. Something that, in my eyes, and those of the Ones who could See, like Twm and Taid and me, swirled and glowed and shone with all the shades of blue that the universe could muster, and then some. Sky, aquamarine, turquoise, gentian, bluebell, forget-me-not, moonlight-on-snow, deep sea, pale shallows, sapphire, all constantly moving and shifting and changing, like a film of blue oil on clear water.

The Sky-Egg.

The magical Sign that the Sea-King's Daughter had given me, her own twenty-first century incarnation, to keep forever.

I opened the drawer and lifted out the flower-bedecked box that had once held Belgian chocolates and now held the Sky-Egg. Ice frosted the outside of the box, and the silk scarf that covered it was brittle with cold.

The Sky-Egg had been warm to touch since the first time I had held it between my hands, awe-struck and delighted. Now it was giving off waves of cold so intense that my teeth chattered and goose-bumps popped out on my arms.

I opened the box. The Sky-Egg had no ice on its surface, but when I lifted it out, it felt like holding a dry ice-cube. My fingers numbed almost instantly, and I laid the beautiful thing back in the nest of cotton wool I'd made to keep it safe on the journey from Wales. I closed the box, closed the drawer, and sat, draped in my duvet, on the edge of the frilly bed, utterly mystified.

I needed to speak to Twm. The problem was that I couldn't phone him directly, there was no phone in the cottage that he shared with his Taid and Cei, his little brother, so I'd have to phone Mom and Dad and ask them to ask Twm to be on the call-box by the post office in Pontpentre-dŵr at a particular time. Kind of drawn-out and inconvenient, but the only way. Fortunately Mom had given me a phone card so I could call whenever I felt homesick or needed a ten-minute fix of family.

Monsieur and Madame had gone to bed, and I could hear Marie-Claire fussing about in her room next door. I needed to be very, very quiet.

I dialled the Toll House. It rang for ages before Dad, sounding real sleepy and none too pleased, picked up.

'Whozat?' he mumbled. 'Wozmarra?'

'Hi, Dad. It's me.'

'Catrin? What's wrong, honey? Are you ill?'

'No, Dad. I'm fine, really I am. I know it's kinda late, but I need to speak to Twm, like, now. It's real, real important, Dad. Could you go get him to wait by the call-box in the village so I –'

'What? You got me out of bed so you could talk to Twm? Dream on, Catrin, you must be mad if you think I'm going out at this time of night on a dumb whim!'

'No, Dad! It isn't like that. It's, like real –'

'Honey, however important you think it is, I'm sure it can wait until morning. I'll stop by the cottage on my way to the office tomorrow, I promise. But Twm's gonna be in bed asleep right now, and no way am I disturbing him or his Taid, you hear? Now go to bed, honey. I'll speak to you tomorrow. Night, sweetheart.'

'But Dad –!'

'Night, sugar-plum. I'll call you tomorrow. We'll have a real good chin-wag then, OK?' The receiver clicked down. I felt so frustrated I could have screamed. What now? I knew I couldn't possibly sleep until I'd spoken to Twm.

Then I had an idea. I fished out my diary from the bottom of the sock drawer. There it was; the number of the callbox in the village. I shut my eyes and said a little prayer, then dialled. The phone rang, and I pictured the little red box with the glass sides outside the village shop-cum-post office. Then someone picked up the receiver at the other end.

'Catrin? Is that you? It's me, Twm.'

CHAPTER TWO

I tell you, I was so relieved to hear his voice I gabbled at him like a moron. 'Oh, Twm, wow! How did you know I wanted to speak to you? This is, like so totally, majorly cool, I –'

'Shut up, Catrin. Listen, will you?'

'Oh, sure, sorry, Twm, but it's like –'

'Shut *up*, Catrin. Just *listen.*'

'Sorry. OK, right, I'm listening.'

'You have to get back here. It's really, really important that you come back, right now.'

'But I –'

'*Now*, Catrin.'

'I can't, Twm! I have to stay here another two months, you know that.'

'You aren't listening to me. They're back.'

'Back? Who?'

'The Spoilers. Oh, not Humphreys and Mrs Prosser, they're still running around squeaking, but Mrs Gwynne-Davies and Miss Critchett. Them. Which means there must be another two of them around somewhere. There are always four, remember?'

I remembered. I remembered Taid turning Humphreys, Mrs Gwynne-Davies's chauffeur and Mrs Prosser, the unpleasant old woman, into rats, but the other two had made themselves scarce after what happened. Now, apparently, they were back.

'So something's gonna happen, right, Twm?' I said.

'Yes. I think it may have started. But you have to get here. We need you, and we need the Signs.'

'But Twm, we only have the Sky Egg! We gave the other Signs back to the Sea-King's Daughter.'

'I know that, *twpsyn*, but we know where to find them, don't we? But you have to be here so we can get hold of them. So just come home, all right? Look, I've got to go.'

'But Twm –'

Too late. He'd hung up.

Well, and wasn't that just great? Here was I in a foreign country being ordered to get back home. Like, how? Sure, Monsieur and Madame would drive me to the ferryport or stick me on a plane home and pay for the ticket. Not. So what was I going to do?

I put the phone down and sat, stunned, on the edge of the bed in my freezing room. Brr. It'd be good to get home just to warm up. Except I'd have to take the icy Sky Egg with me. How could I get home? I had just about enough euros to take a cab to the airport, but that was it.

Then, strangely, my eye fell on the little purple leather purse Mom had hidden in my luggage before I left. Cute gift, but I never carry a purse. That's what pockets are for, right? I'd never even opened it. I don't *do* purses, and I thought Mom knew that. It was still hanging on a hook on the back of the door right where I'd put it when I unpacked it four months ago. So why was I kind of *noticing* it now? Had to be a reason, yeah?

I got up and unhooked it, opened it. Inside was an envelope. It had my name on it. Inside was a note in Mom's handwriting.

Sweetheart, it said, *I know you don't want to go to France right now, but in time you'll come to see that you've been given a huge advantage. Grab it with both hands, baby, because you'll thank me later on. Not to say I won't miss you like crazy, Cat! Here's something for you. Think of it as mad-money. Go buy yourself something when you feel blue, OK?*

It was signed, *all my love, Mom.*

The note was wrapped around a Visa card, in my name. A huge grin spread across my face. Saved! I was out of here, like, now!

I hastily scribbled a note to Madame and left it on my pillow, changed into Levis and a sweatshirt, put on my Timberlands, packed the Sky Egg in my backpack, grabbed my fleece hoodie, and headed for Way Out. I slithered noiselessly downstairs, unchained the front door and clicked it silently behind me. The path to the main road was shadowy between the trees, and there was no way anyone was going to see me. The whole house was asleep.

The whole *house* was, yeah. Just as I turned from silently latching the garden gate, I bumped into someone.

'Oh, *mer-*' Marie-Claire stopped herself swearing just in time. 'Catrreen, whair do you go at zis time of night?' A tall male figure was disappearing down the road as fast as his legs would take him.

'Home,' I said, shortly.

'But you can't. Maman she will worry. I shall go and tell 'er, now. You must come wiz me. You are vairy notty.'

'No way, Marie-Claire. Forget it. Besides, if you go in and wake Madame, then I shall just have to tell her that you were out here necking with Jean-Daniel, which is also vairy notty, right? And didn't I hear you say goodnight and go to bed a while ago? Did you sneak out your window, Marie-Claire? Shame on you!'

'Zat is none of your *affaire,* Catrreen. I shall not answer you. You must not tell Maman. I forbeed eet.'

'I won't tell Maman if you won't tell Maman – at least until the morning. Anyhow, I left a note. She'll know where I've gone. But I'm going home.'

'But 'ow? You can 'ardly swim zer shannel.'

I didn't tell her I could have, actually, because I'm the Sea Girl. I might have, except my sense of direction is so lousy I'd probably have ended up in Norway or someplace instead of Cardigan Bay.

'Never mind how. I just am. I'm out of here. And you better keep your mouth shut until morning, Marie-Claire, or else!'

I sprinted down the road and into the town. There had to be a cab around someplace, right? There was. I found one cruising downtown, through the dark streets between the shopfronts. He didn't see me at first, I had to kind of hurl myself in front of him to make him notice me. He slammed on his brakes and I climbed in the backseat.

'*Le Aeroport, s'il vous plait,*' I said. He didn't ask

questions, he just drove, a cigarette dangling precariously from the corner of his mouth, his eyes squinting round the smelly smoke, and one arm out the window. He pulled up outside the automatic doors to the airport concourse, told me the fare and held out his hand for me to count euros and bits of euros into it. I managed a tip, too.

'*Merci,*' he said, '*bon voyage,*' and drove off. Now, that was way cool. In the States cabdrivers mostly talk you to death and want to know your whole life story – or they tell you theirs.

At the ticket desk, I used the credit card to buy a ticket on the next flight to Cardiff – no problem there. I'd make it home somehow, though I wasn't sure how! I didn't have any British money, and not too many euros, but I could phone home, maybe. I winced. Mom and Dad were going to be so mad at me!

My flight left in two hours, so I found a chair in an unobtrusive corner and tried to sleep. I couldn't, of course, what with the lights, the constant traffic of feet and conversation and bings and bongs and bellows from the tannoy system. At last my flight was called and before long I was airborne. My stomach churned, half happy, half scared. It felt great leaving France behind and knowing I was going home. I just hoped I could get to Mom and Dad to reassure them before Monsieur and Madame found my note. They wouldn't, until morning when I didn't appear for *petit dejeuner*, but all the same . . .

As soon as we landed, I hit the bank of telephones

in the concourse. First call, Twm's callbox, but there was no reply. Second call, a wake-up call for Mom and Dad, was to the Toll House. To my surprise, the phone was snatched up instantly.

'Hello? Hello? Who is it?'

'Hi, Mom, it's me, Catrin.'

'Catrin! Where are you? We've been out of our heads with worry!'

'Why?' Dumb thing to say, Catrin.

'Why? *Why?* Madame telephones us at three a.m. to say you've gone missing and you ask why we're worried? I do not *believe* you, Catrin Rhys Morgan!'

'Madame didn't –' I got this sudden vision of my Mom. I just *knew* that the end of her nose had gone white, which was a sure sign she was so mad she was about to spontaneously combust, so I wisely shut up. 'Look, Mom, I'm at Cardiff airport. Can you or Dad come get me?'

'Dad will be there as soon as he can. Oh, thank God you're OK. You just wait until you get home, Catrin! I am gonna ground you until you're too old to care! Now you go right to the Information Desk and you stay there until you see the whites of your Dad's eyes. Don't you dare move, Catrin Rhys Morgan!'

Well, I'd expected something like that. Oh, boy, was Dad mad. He raged at me for about the first ten miles, muttered at me for the next five, and then calmed down some. Finally, when he'd run out of all the things he was gonna do to me, he asked the question.

'Why, Catrin?'

'Twm needs me, Dad. He says it's urgent.'

'Twm! I should have known that boy was in there someplace. And you wonder why we sent you to France in the first place.'

That stopped me. 'To learn French. For my education, right, Dad? That's what you said.'

Dad shut up. I stared at him, and then I realised. 'You and Mom sent me to France because of *Twm*?' I howled. 'Why?'

'You were getting too intense. These boy and girl things don't always pan out when you're so young, honey,' he said sympathetically.

'Boy-and-girl thing? There was no boy and girl thing! Twm and I are just real good friends with a whole lot in common, Dad. Good grief! He's never even kissed me for gosh's sake!'

'He hasn't?' He took his eyes off the road and stared at me. 'Honest?'

'Honest.'

'Well.' He grinned. 'I told your Mom she was over-reacting.'

I was starting to get real mad. 'You mean you sent me all the way to France for six whole months –'

'Four. It's only April, and you're back.'

'Whatever. You sent me because you thought I was having a Thing with Twm? I do not believe it!'

Dad was getting uncomfortable now, so I pressed home my advantage.

'I cannot believe that you didn't even discuss this with me! What happened to "sharing stuff with the family", Dad? What happened to "keeping lines of communication open with our children", Dad? What happened to "nothing's so bad we can't discuss it," Dad? Do you know what it's been *like* in La Rochelle?'

'Different, I would have thought,' he said, rallying for a comeback.

'Yeah, if your idea of different is being forced to try on frilly dresses with a complete dork, and having to do it in a foreign language,' I said, bitterly. 'And they eat such weird stuff, Dad! If it hadn't been for Big Macs I'd have died.'

He was laughing now, and I think he'd forgiven me already. Just Mom to go.

What was I thinking? 'Just Mom' indeed!

Aaaaargh!

CHAPTER THREE

My Mom was so mad her whole face was white, not just her nose. Scary. She started in right as I walked through the door of the Toll House. I pasted a big smile on my face, kind of hoping to divert the explosion before it started, but no way was that gonna work.

'I am so angry, Catrin! I can't believe you'd do such a thing! You're sixteen, and you run away from your host family on a hare-brained jaunt across Europe! Didn't you realise how worried we'd be?'

'I –'

'Don't interrupt! When Madame phoned this morning I was so scared I almost had a heart attack. Don't you realise what could have happened to you? How dangerous it is for a girl of your age to take off on her own without telling anyone?'

'But –'

'I said, don't interrupt. Anything at all could have happened. You might be lying dead in a ditch right now!'

'I –'

'I said, don't interrupt! Now, what have you got to say for yourself?'

Logical, right? Don't interrupt, but speak up. I guess Mom wasn't feeling too rational right then. I took a deep breath. 'Well, in the first place, I thought I'd get home before Madame woke up and found my note. And you knew I was coming, anyhow, Mom! I said in the note.'

'Note? What note? Madame didn't mention any note. Marie-Claire woke her and Monsieur up in the early hours of the morning to tell them that your bed was empty and you'd disappeared! They raised the gendarmes to look for you, Catrin! They've been scouring La Rochelle for you all night!'

'That rotten little – look, Mom, I did so leave a note, and Marie-Claire knew it. As I was going out the front, she was coming back in! She'd sneaked out to be with that dorkish boyfriend of hers. She didn't mention that, did she, when she dumped me in it?'

'Is this true? You really left a note?'

'Sure I did. You think I'd just, like, take off and leave everyone to worry about me? You brought me up better than that, Mom!'

'I certainly thought I had.' The white was beginning to die back, now. Only the tip of her nose was frostbitten. 'But why couldn't you wait a while to come home, honey? And you left all your stuff behind! It's only two months, now, and you were doing so well with your French. Madame is going to have to pack all your things and ship them over here.'

I started to open my mouth, tell her how I'd spoken to Twm, how he needed me, but then my common sense kicked in. I didn't want the white creeping back, did I? And I wanted to see Twm, right? No way did I want to be grounded! I needed my freedom. So, OK, so maybe I was just a teensy bit crafty . . .

'Oh, Mom, I was just so homesick! I couldn't sleep, and I hated the food, and Marie-Claire, oh, she's such a creep!'

'Hmm. Well, not showing her Mom your note, that was sneaky, I'll admit. But all the same . . .'

'And I missed you and Daddy, Mommy. And Jake. I don't like to be so far away from my family. I was real lonesome and homesick and miserable.'

The white was gone, even from the end of her nose. I'd called her Mommy, right, and that like always, but always, does the trick. Sneaky, but there are times when a girl has to do such stuff to get herself off the hook. It worked. She opened her arms and gathered me in for a huge hug. Dad, who'd been hiding in the kitchen, came in and joined it, and behind his back, standing on the stairs, I saw my little brother Jake. Did he come and join in the happy family reunion Hug? No way. He stayed where he was and stuck his finger down his throat, pretending to barf. I crossed my eyes and stuck out my tongue.

Madoc, my little border collie cross, stood in the doorway, his light, light, eyes-that-have-seen-the-wind staring in disbelief, then with a joyful whine he launched himself at my legs. I bent down and allowed myself to be comprehensively washed by a flailing red tongue. Looked like everyone was pleased to have me back.

'I've already telephoned Madame to tell her you're safe,' Mom said, releasing me and pulling a tissue from a box to wipe her eyes. 'But I think I'll phone her back and suggest she asks Marie-Claire what happened to the note you left, and also what Marie-Claire was doing out in the middle of the night.'

'Before you do that, Mom,' I said, holding up a hand, 'can I take it I'm not gonna have to go back?'

Mom and Dad exchanged glances. 'I guess not, honey,' Dad said. 'If you were so homesick in La Rochelle, it would be too cruel to make you go back.'

Mom nodded, and started puddling up again. She scuttled into the kitchen and started rattling skillets and plopping gas. Good. I could do with some breakfast. Then I noticed Dad's face. He was grinning from ear to ear, and shaking his head. He knew perfectly well that I'd twisted Mom round my little finger, just as I'd twisted him round in the car.

Parents! Now I had guilt! One way or another, they get you every time, right?

Oh, it was so cool to be home! To look out of my bedroom window and see the churning grey mass of Cardigan Bay, hear the wind howling around the slate roof and bending the trees over at right-angles, listen to the rain splattering on the windows . . .

After bacon, egg and field mushrooms Jake had picked the day before, I had a quick shower, changed, and headed off to the village on my bike, the backpack containing the Sky Egg cold against my back. Luckily the rain had quit, so the ride wasn't too awful. I skidded to a halt in front of the cottage and rapped on the stable door. The top half opened, and Taid's head poked out.

'Catrin, *cariad! O, croeso, croeso!*' he smiled.

'Twm, *bachgen*, look who has come home! Come in, *ferch, dewch i mewn.*'

A thunder of feet on the stairs and there was Twm, a great grin splitting his face. I hadn't expected him to have changed quite so much in four months: he was close on six feet tall now, and his light brown hair was streaked with sun and salt. His pale blue eyes shone in his brown face.

'About blooming time, too!' he said, flinging open the bottom half of the door and hauling me into a huge hug.

Ooh, I was glad my Mom and Dad didn't see *that*. They'd have packed me straight off to moulder in Massachusetts, if they had! And you know what? I enjoyed it. He smelled of salt and the sea, and he was warm and solid and *good*.

'So,' I said, pushing him away and plonking myself down on my usual stool at Taid's feet, 'what's going on?'

'Cup of tea, first,' Taid said, getting up and bustling around with the kettle on the black hob of the fire. 'And a bit of nice *bara brith gyda menyn.*'

So tea and buttered *bara brith* it was. I munched while Twm explained.

'It's the wild creatures, Catrin,' he began. 'For weeks now I've noticed things. The bees, for a start. They are all unsettled and restive and this time of year, they shouldn't be. I don't know what's happening, and that's why you had to come back. The wild things need us, Catrin. For some reason I can't help them.'

44

Now, you may think it's weird to read of someone talking to bees, and I'll agree that yes, it probably sounds that way. But not if you're Twm, who can talk to just about everything that's wild, and does. He's special, Twm is. He's descended from Merlin, you know, the Magician, *that* Merlin, and his Mom – well, his Mom communicates with him by way of a bowl full of water. Oh, never mind. You'll catch up as we go along, I guess.

'And the sea-creatures are unhappy, too. I was out in my boat yesterday, and the seals didn't come. You know they always come to me, Catrin, you know they do, but yesterday I didn't see even one.' He shoved his fingers through his hair, got up and paced. 'But how can I help them when I don't know what's wrong? The dolphin I sent to find you helped, but I'm sure there's something wrong there, too. They're uneasy as well. It must be the Spoilers. They sense them.'

'How can we find out?' I asked. 'What can we do? Have you asked your Mom?'

Taid sighed. 'Oh, we've tried, *ferch*, over and over we have tried, but we can't reach her. Perhaps now you are home . . .'

'We could try, Taid, but I've got a feeling that we won't be able to do anything until we've got all the Signs back,' Twm said.

That reminded me. 'I brought the Sky Egg,' I said, reaching for my pack. 'Something real weird is happening to it. Ever since the day I found it in Cardigan Market, in the shop that wasn't there, it has been warm, like body-temperature, you know? Now, suddenly, it's cold as ice. Feel.' I passed the icy Egg to Taid, and saw the blood fade away from the wrinkled old hands as the cold got to him.

'*Rhyfeddol!*' Taid said, 'Remarkable! Take it, Twm! You know what this means?'

Twm nodded, slowly. 'It means we have to move fast, find the other signs.'

'What are you guys talking about?' I yelped. 'What does it mean, the Egg being cold? Will you please tell me?'

'The Sky Egg,' Taid said slowly, 'is the last remaining egg of the last dragon ever to live in the whole wide world. Dragons are cold-blooded creatures, but when the time is not right for them, their eggs are warm, like the Sky Egg used to be when you had it here before. But when they are preparing to hatch, the eggs become as cold as ice – and then, just before the baby dragon bursts out of the egg, the egg becomes so hot that it would burn your hands if you touched it.'

'You mean,' I said, staring at the beautiful blue Sky Egg in Twm's hands, 'you mean that's a *dragon's egg* and it's going to *hatch?*'

Taid smiled. 'Possibly. But there is another reason why the Egg is cold. It could be a warning of danger. The vibrations that danger sets up in nature would set off the protective coating of the Egg, the one that the mother dragon leaves to safeguard the eggs when she isn't around. The Egg won't hatch until it's ready, and since this one has been dormant for a couple of thousand years, then I'd say we've got a bit to wait, yet. I'm more inclined to think it's danger that's cooled this egg down. This is no fit place for a baby dragon, no, no place at all, and besides it will not have a mother if it comes now.'

I stared at Twm and Taid, trying to get my head round this. Before I came to Wales, I would probably have sent for the nice guys in the white coats, and hustled the pair of them off to the Funny Farm, but this was Wales, and somehow the totally unbelievable became only too believable here.

'So, what's our next step, then?' I asked.

'Contact my Mam,' Twm said, 'or try to, anyway.'

He fetched the beautiful, polished wooden bowl from the big dresser against the wall, and poured some leaves into it from a little leather bag. He set fire to the leaves with an ember from the always-burning fire, and when the flames had died down and the ashes had cooled, he mashed up the remains and smeared the black ash around the rim of the bowl. He filled the bowl with clear water, and set it on a low table between him and Taid. Then we waited for the water to become completely still.

Perhaps because of the rim of ash, perhaps because of the darkness that was always present in the little cottage, even at noon on the brightest day, the water was black as ebony. Our three faces, bent over the bowl, were reflected in it, but that wasn't what we were waiting to see. Twm blew softly on the surface, which rippled under his breath and stilled again.

'She's not coming, Taid,' he said, sadly.

'Yes, she is,' I said. 'There she is! I can see her!'

And there she was, Twm's mother, her pale face floating like a dream in the depths of the bowl, her hair blowing softly about her face, a welcoming smile on her red lips. I heard her voice in my head.

'Catrin, you've come home! There is so much work to be done, *Ferch y Môr,* so much danger. First, you must find the Signs. You have the Sky Egg. Keep it safe. Don't let the Spoilers find it. Keep it with you, always. When you have found the other Signs, then you will know.'

'Know what?'

'I can't tell you, I don't know. I'm trying to find out, but something is hindering me. Beware of the Spoilers. Two of them you know, but there are always four. They are . . .'

'What?'

But the surface of the bowl was misting, and the face shimmered and was gone.

CHAPTER FOUR

'Rats! She's gone!' I said, slumping back on the stool again.

'You saw her?' Twm said. 'Why couldn't I, then?'

I shrugged.

'What did she say?' Taid asked.

Twm busied himself emptying the bowl.

'She said we have to find the other Signs, first off. And she said we have to beware of the Spoilers. She was about to tell me who they were, I guess, but then we lost contact before she could. She said something's like, blocking her. Maybe that's why she couldn't talk to you, Twm. The Spoilers know about you, but I guess maybe they think I'm still in France.' I groaned. 'So now we don't know who it is we're looking for, even. It'll be like finding a needle in a haystack, trying to find the Spoilers.'

'Oh, you'll probably recognise them if you meet them,' Taid said. 'But if she says the first thing you've got to do is find the other Signs, then you'd better start looking.'

'But we know where they are,' I said. 'We gave them back to the Sea Girl, all but the Sky Egg, and now they're at the bottom of the ocean. So how are we to get them back?'

'Same way as we returned them,' Twm said. 'At least we don't have to go all over the place trying to track them down this time.'

'Oh, right,' I said, 'they're about a mile down in Cardigan Bay. We'll just swim out and get them, shall we?'

'No. We'll take my boat. *Then* we'll swim,' Twm said calmly.

Then I remembered that of course, I can do stuff like that. I am the Sea Girl, right?

'You'd better take the iron box with you, Twm,' Taid reminded his grandson. 'Try putting the Earthstone in the bottom of the boat and you'll have a longer swim than you bargained for!'

The Earthstone was the Sign that returned to nature everything that had been made by the hand of man. The other Sign was the Sea Harp, a musical instrument so magical that, when its silvery strings were plucked, the music stilled everyone who heard it. They froze, unable to move or speak, until the Harp was played again. And when folks were frozen, whoever was holding the Sky Egg could make them believe anything at all: that Elvis Presley really was alive and serving burgers in Hicksville, USA; or – being serious about it – that something catastrophic really was going to happen unless some key person stepped in to prevent it. As a rule, certain adults tended not to listen to teenagers like Twm and me – that's what we discovered last time we needed to use the Harp and the Egg! So, yeah. We needed all the Signs, like, now!

'Right,' I said. 'When do we go?'

'Now,' Twm said. 'The sooner we start this, the better.'

So, leaving the Egg in Taid's safe keeping, we headed for the shore. As I mentioned earlier, it was kind of windy, not the type of day when the first idea to enter a person's head is, 'wow, what a great day for a nice long trip out to sea in a little boat!' The ocean was tossing about enthusiastically and, as a result, so was Twm's dinghy. It went uuuup and doooown, uuuup and doooown. It wasn't real comfortable, but at least I didn't get seasick any more. Was a time I did, but being the Sea Girl seems to have cured all that. Twm used his little outboard motor to take us out into the bay, chugged past the crouching hump of the island and out to sea. Then he cut the engine, got the iron box out of his backpack, took off his waterproof jacket, jeans, sweatshirt and boots, and lowered himself over the side in his swimtrunks. I dipped my hand in the water, and it was as cold as it looked . . .

'Twm, I don't have a swimsuit on.'

'What's your point, Catrin? You're wearing something, aren't you?'

'Of course. But –'

'Then get in here. Come on, hurry.'

Well, at least I was wearing a decent sports bra and brief set that looked like a bikini, and who was to see anyway? I stripped down and lowered myself gingerly over the side.

'Aaaaah!' I croaked as the water hit my bare belly. 'Aaaah!' It was so cold I couldn't make any noise beyond a whisper.

'Come on. You'll be better underwater,' Twm said, diving down, his bare legs rising above the surface as his head went down. I took a deep breath and followed him, letting it out slowly, a bit nervous about swimming down deep after all this time.

But just as it had before, the Sea Girl part of me took over, and I was soon breathing normally – normally for a Sea Girl under water, that is – in and out, in and out, following Twm down into the depths. The sun followed us down through the water, and strangely, didn't seem to grow any less the deeper we went. I grew more at home in this watery element, and even the cold didn't matter any more: I was at one with the Sea. Down and down we went, and at last, hundreds of metres down, we saw the ghostly outline of Taliesin's tower, the silent bell swaying in the movement of the tide, fish gliding in and out of the flute-like windows. This was where we'd left the Sea Harp and the Earthstone. The Sea King's Daughter had returned the Sky Egg to me to keep, which had seemed right. After all, it had come to me, not the other way about, and we'd had to go look for the other two Signs.

Twm's lithe body turned gracefully in the water as he slipped through a tall window and into the bell-tower. I followed him, heading instinctively for the place where we'd left the other Signs.

They weren't there.

Twm and I searched the bell-tower, sifted through the sand that lay on the floor, but they were gone. He floated in front of me.

'They aren't here!' he said, his voice echoing in my mind rather than my ears.

We searched Taliesin's tower, room by room, but found no trace of either Earthstone or Sea Harp. More towers loomed about us darkly through the water: there were sixteen cities in Cantre'r Gwaelod, and this was only the first. We might be searching for ages.

'No,' Twm's voice cut into my thoughts, 'they won't be in any other tower if they aren't in Taliesin's, I'm sure of that. Taliesin's tower is the only one with enough magic to contain them. Any other tower would have crumbled away. Think about it, Catrin: the Sixteen Cities of Cantre'r Gwaelod were made by the hand of man – they couldn't have lasted, not if the Earthstone was inside them. Only Taliesin's tower could hold it, because he built it with magic so the stones themselves kept the Earthstone in check.'

'So, where?' I asked.

'I don't know. The Sea King's Daughter left them in the bell-tower, next to Taliesin's harp. Perhaps she took them with her.'

'Took them with her? Where did she go? Where could she go – she belongs down here, right?'

'Right, Catrin. But one of the dolphins told me something weird a few weeks ago. I forgot all about it – dolphins are imaginative creatures, and sometimes they make things up. But now I wonder.'

I knew Twm talked to dolphins, so that was no surprise. But dolphins making stuff up? 'You're putting me on, right?' I said uncertainly. 'About the dolphins.'

'What, being imaginative? Of course I'm not.' He scowled at me. 'You know perfectly well that dolphins' brains are as big as ours – we're imaginative, why shouldn't they be? Honestly, you and your prejudices.'

Stung, I retorted, 'I am not either prejudiced! I just never thought of dolphins being anything other than dolphins, I guess. Anyhow, what was it the dolphin told you?'

'He said that the Sea Girl had left the ocean – gone a-dusty, was the way he put it. I couldn't imagine her doing that, so I forgot all about it until now.'

'She's on land? Why?'

'According to the dolphin, she ran away because she fell in love with a fisherman. It often happens with mermaids, but they usually don't get far because of the tail problem, and sometimes seals take human form when they fall in love. Silkies, they're called then. But the Sea Girl, being half-human anyway, would be able to go ashore easily.'

I was busy boggling, trying to get to grips with the concept and not succeeding real well.

'Anyway,' my companion said, slipping through the door of Taliesin's tower, 'I suppose we'd better think again. If she's on shore, then we'd better find her and hope she's got the Signs with her. Because if her father has them, we could have problems.'

'Her – father?' I swam after him, 'she has a *father*?'

'Well, yes, Catrin. That's why she's called the Sea King's *Daughter*.'

'But if she's hundreds of years old, what does that make him?'

'It makes him the Sea King, that's what. And trust me, he's someone we don't want to tangle with if we can help it. In fact, I think we should get away from here as soon as we can. We don't want to attract his attention.'

'How would we do that?'

'Just being here should do it. And I've a horrible feeling we already have.'

'How do you –'

Then I noticed the shark . . .

My shriek of terror blasted a column of bubbles out of my mouth, twinkling up through the water. Twm grabbed my arm to calm me down, but it was too late: if the sharks hadn't seen us already, they certainly had now. Tapered tails flicked, and grey, flattened heads with cold, dead eyes turned towards us.

'Keep calm, now, Catrin,' Twm hissed. 'Don't make any sudden moves, all right?'

'All r-r-r-ight? Are you mad? Those are *sharks*, Twm! Like, chomp-up city! And you want me to stay calm? D-d-dream on!'

'They're only watching us, Catrin. They won't kill us. They're not man-eaters.'

'How do you know? Maybe they're hungry for us!' One of the sharks swam real close and opened its mouth. 'Will you look at those teeth! Oh, man! If he decided to take a nibble at me he'd do more than just give me a nasty suck.'

'Perhaps the Sea King sent them, Catrin, to warn us off.'

'Consider me warned. I really, really wanna get in the boat now, Twm. But they're between us and it? Oh, shoot! What if they bring on their big brothers?'

'Stop panicking and follow me, Catrin.'

I wasn't convinced, but with Twm hanging on tight to my hand I had no option but to go. I wanted to shut my eyes, but I was too scared to not look.

The sharks twitched their tails and arrowed through the water, eight of them. They looked like every shark nightmare I'd had since seeing *Jaws* when I was way too young to see it, thanks to a babysitter who was more interested in the boyfriend she smuggled in than what we kids were watching on TV in the den.

We swam up towards the surface, and they split into two lines of four, one each side of us, and kind of escorted us upward. They say sharks are attracted by the smell of fear, so I wouldn't have been surprised if every shark in the ocean wasn't swimming our way! I was so scared I couldn't think. Twm kept tight hold of my hand and towed me behind him, his head up, aiming for the brightness above. Then, they flicked above us and peeled off, allowing us to regain the safety of the boat. By the time we reached it, I was clutching Twm's hand so tight I was probably cutting off his circulation.

Then my hands were grabbing on to warm wood, and Twm was boosting me up.

CHAPTER FIVE

I collapsed in a whimpering heap on the bottom of the boat. Twm shoved himself up on the edge and tossed me a towel from his backpack. My teeth were chattering with pure terror. I quaked as I dried myself and dressed over my soggy underwear.

Twm fired up the outboard and turned the boat back to shore, his brown skin glistening with droplets of water.

'I have never been so glad to get out of the water, Twm! Those sharks – oh, wow. That was mega-scary, Twm!'

'Honestly, they weren't going to harm us, Catrin, there was no need to be frightened.'

'All the same, I'm real glad to be out of there.' I looked round anxiously, expecting to see a dorsal fin cut the surface of the sea, but it was calm and blue and innocuous looking. Nothing betrayed the terror beneath.

'So, we have to find the Sea Girl, I guess. Question is, where do we start looking?'

'At least we know it's a fisherman she's fallen in love with – that narrows it down.'

'Oh yeah, sure. To about a million miles of Welsh coastline, Twm! Like, no sweat!'

He glanced at me and grinned. 'Oh, it isn't going to be too hard to find her. After all, I've got my special agents, haven't I?'

'Special agents? What special agents?'

'The birds, the bees, the fish. They go everywhere, so I've got a network of eyes and ears covering the whole of Wales. If I ask them to look, then they'll find her if she's out there to find.'

I brightened. 'Oh, cool. Then we just go where she's at, ask her for the Signs, and everything'll be fine and dandy?'

'Not exactly. Finding the Signs is only the beginning, isn't it? We still have to find out why we need them.'

'Oh. Yes. I'd forgotten that. And who the new Spoilers are, too.'

'Exactly. So it isn't going to be that easy. I just hope whatever it is is something that we are able to fix – and quickly.'

'Can I ask a dumb question?'

'If it isn't too dumb.'

'How come the Sea Girl is still around? I'm supposed to be her reincarnation, right? She looks like me, doesn't she? So why are there two of us at once? If a person is a reincarnation, the first version gets to die, right?'

'Not always. Old Ones don't die. They change, become part of nature – like the Sea Girl has, more an element than a person and sometimes she has a tail, sometimes not, like now. I'm not sure exactly how it works, Catrin. All I know is that you are the Sea Girl, and so is she. You and she share the same spirit.'

'I'm having kind of a lot of trouble understanding this. How can I be part of her spirit when I'm me?'

'Because like her, you're part human, and you're an Old One too. The Sea Girl is an Old One, whatever incarnation she's in, so it follows that you must be, too.'

'Do you think there may be other Sea Girls we don't know about?'

'I don't think so, no.'

I sighed. 'I can't get my head round this Old One stuff. I was born and raised in Pittsburgh, Pennsylvania. I'm sixteen, and I'm supposed to get around three score years and ten same as every other guy. I don't get it.'

Twm grinned. 'Why ever not? Even Old Ones have to start somewhere. I've only been here – oh, how long? Must be about two hundred and seventy years, now.'

'Pull the other one, Twm. It's got bells on. They go ding-a-ling, just like you.'

He shrugged. 'Please yourself. All the same, it's true. You'll be around a lot longer than you think.'

I didn't believe him, naturally. I could tell when I was being led down the garden path! 'Yeah, right,' I said, and shifted my rear end on the wooden seat as we approached the beach.

We hauled the boat up above the highwater mark and Twm padlocked the outboard motor. 'Don't usually bother with this,' he muttered. 'Nobody dishonest enough to steal a boat in Pontpentre-dŵr, but with the Spoilers around, I'm not taking any chances. In a way, I wish we could meet them, get it over with. Once we've identified them, at least we'll be able to keep an eye on what they're doing.'

We left the beach and walked the mile or so into the village where I'd left my bike.

'I guess I'd better go home, Twm,' I said reluctantly. 'Mom and Dad haven't seen me for four months, and I need to spend some time with them. But don't go looking for the Sea Girl without me, promise?'

'I promise. I have to ask my friends to start looking, anyway. I'll talk to Taid tonight, and give you a ring tomorrow morning. Take care, Catrin. Don't talk to any strangers on the way home.'

'I won't.' I swung my leg over the saddle and pedalled off, over the little bridge and down the road towards the Toll House. Oh, it was so good to be home. Half way home I remembered I'd left the Sky Egg with Taid: never mind, he'd take care of it until I could get it back. I'd kind of forgotten how important it was until now. After the last adventure, and while I was in France, it was just a beautiful object. I never dreamed I might need to use it again.

Mom was baking cookies in the kitchen when I arrived. I sniffed appreciatively: chocolate chip, unless my nose was out of practice from all that French cooking! I lifted the tea-towel covering them. I was right: I stole one and stood beside Mom nibbling it as she wielded the cookie-cutter.

'Don't eat too many of those, honey. I'm doing my special meatloaf for dinner, with green beans, and you don't want to spoil your appetite.'

'Wow! Special meatloaf! Oh, far out! And all in my honour!'

'Well, partly in your honour, Catrin. We have company tonight.'

'We do? Who?'

'Oh, one of the Directors from Dad's parent company in Pittsburgh is over for a month or two to see how the factory is coming along. Dad says it's coming along just fine without any need for the brass from Stateside visiting, but hey, those guys don't believe a thing unless they can see it, right?

'I guess so. Where's Jake?'

'Where else? Off with Cei. The two of them are inseparable these days – I barely see him between sun-up and sundown.'

I finished my cookie and took another, fending off Mom's playful slap. 'Just one more, Mom? I'm starving. I might die if I have to wait until dinner.'

Mom looked at her watch. 'Dad will be home at about six, and it's nearly four now. Could you set the table, honey, before you go upstairs to shower and change into something pretty?'

Which was Mom's subtle way of telling me she wanted me looking like a girl at dinner, not a salty somebody who'd spent the afternoon messing about in a boat.

I set the table with the best china and silverware, and then went upstairs to shower. I opened my wardrobe to find something to wear: I'd lost some weight in France despite all that food, and in the end had to settle for a pair of navy wide-legged linen trousers and a white t-shirt – tidy casual, I guess. I was slipping my toes into a pair of flat Vans when I

61

heard Dad's key in the front door, and Mom's voice welcoming our guest.

Actually, I could have done without spending my first real evening home with some boring old guy from the US. I wanted to catch up with family stuff, and you can't talk properly with a stranger at the table.

I brushed on some mascara, half-listening to Dad and Mom downstairs. An unfamiliar voice was rumbling in the background. The smell of meatloaf wafting up the stairs was making my tummy rumble, despite the chocolate chip cookies, and I decided the faster I got myself downstairs, the faster I'd get fed, so I ran down.

Like, Big Mistake. I tripped half way down, my feet went from under me, and I went base-over-apex all the way down the stairs and landed in a heap by the Welsh dresser in the corner.

'Ow!' I moaned, sitting up and rubbing my elbow. Mom came running out of the sitting room, closely followed by Dad.

'Oh, honey, did you trip?' Mom fussed, while Dad helped me up.

'No, Mom, I flew, just for the adventure factor, you know,' I said, feeling undignified. 'Like, yeah, Mom. Of course I tripped!'

Someone appeared in the doorway behind Mom. My mouth fell open in surprise. He was tall, and whatever else he looked like, he didn't look a whole lot like Takahashi Top Brass. No way.

For a start, he wore a Pittsburgh Steelers t-shirt

with blue jeans, not a dark suit and tie. He also had braids, tied with leather strings. Around his forehead was a narrow band of bright fabric, and around his neck hung a dream-catcher on a thong.

'Meet my elegant daughter,' Dad said, grinning. 'Catrin, this is Walter-He-Who-Flies-With-Eagles. Walt for short.'

'P-pleased to meet you,' I mumbled, sticking out my hand. He took it and shook it gravely. His hand was large and brown and warm and dry and felt kind of reassuring, like he wasn't dying to crack up laughing at me. 'Cool name!'

'What, Walt?' he said, and grinned. 'Hope you didn't hurt yourself too bad. I find it's less painful to walk down stairs than fly.'

'What about the eagles?' I shot back.

'They don't have much use for stairs.'

I grinned. I decided I liked him.

My brother Jake was gazing at our guest with what was, unmistakably, hero-worship written all over his face. 'He's a real Red Indian, Catty!' he whispered.

'Native American, dork,' I whispered back. 'You know what? I guessed! The braids and stuff kind of gave it away.'

'Oh, you think you're so smart!' he muttered.

'That's because I am, lamebrain,' I retorted.

'So smart you fell downstairs, right?'

'Children!' Mom chided. 'Manners!'

'Sorry,' I said. 'He's just such a nerd, Mom.'

'I am not!'

'Jake! Quiet!' Dad roared, and my brother

subsided. Behind our guest's back I stuck my tongue out. Round one to me!

'Shall we eat dinner?' Mom said, deftly blocking the dining room doorway against Madoc. He likes to sit beneath the table while we eat, and even though we aren't allowed to feed him while we're eating, that doesn't stop him asking.

Mom wisely put Jake and me at opposite ends of the table so we couldn't kick each other. It was so good to be home!

CHAPTER SIX

Mom cut the meatloaf and passed the plates round. She'd done potatoes baked in their jackets, and the smell of real, American food made my eyes water, as well as my mouth.

Walt was sitting next to me, so I passed him the green beans and filled his water glass for him. Dad had already poured wine for the grown-ups, and I was allowed some too, although Jake complained. He still didn't get any, though, so ha! When we were all served we ate in silence for a while until our appetites were slightly blunted – you know that good feeling when you're real hungry and nothing is more important than getting food inside you?

Then Dad took a swallow of wine. 'So, Walt. What do you think of Wales?'

'What I've seen of it, I like. A guy doesn't get to see too much from an airplane, though. It's all real quaint. Kind of reminds me of the reservation.'

'Wales is like a *reservation*?' It was out before I could stop myself.

'Yeah, kinda. My Mom and Dad still live on the Iroquois reservation back home, and it has that same kind of closed-in environment, a little country inside a bigger one. I confess I didn't know until I'd gotten here that Wales is different than England.'

'Ooh, yes!' I said. 'For Pete's sake don't go calling

this place "England". Wales is like, so, so different. Wales is cool.'

'So I understand. You like living here, Catrin? You made any new buddies?'

'Some. My special friend is Twm. He lives here and we kind of got to know each other when some stuff happened.'

Walt raised an eyebrow. 'Stuff?'

Fortunately Mom jumped in so I didn't have to explain. 'They say Twm's descended from Merlin the Magician, Walt, but then I guess just about every other person is, in Wales! He's a real character, and his Taid – that's his grandpa – is an even bigger one. Twm is very interested in wildlife. He's sort of an unofficial beach warden, and what he doesn't know about birds and animals isn't worth knowing.'

Walt put another forkful of beans into his mouth and chewed thoughtfully. When he'd finished, he said, 'I'd like to meet him. I'm into conservation in a big way. Which is one reason why Mr Takahashi sent me over.'

I pricked up my ears. Mr Takahashi was the Big Boss. 'He sent you?'

Walt grinned. 'Well, officially, yes. I have a feeling that it was actually Mrs Takahashi that did the sending. She and I get on real well, and we have this common interest in preserving the earth for future generations. There's an old Native American saying that goes something like, *you don't own the Earth: you hold it in trust for your children's children's children*. Mrs Takahashi not only knew the saying, she quoted it at me, so I guess she may have had something to do my being here. I was summoned to Takahashi Towers three weeks ago, and when I got there Mr T was in Philadelphia. Mrs T fed me lunch, but she seemed real anxious I shouldn't mention to her husband that we'd met.' He shrugged. 'So when I was asked to come visit Wales, I hopped a plane and here I am.'

I started to ask, 'why –' but Dad fixed me with a look that said, *do not ask questions*, so I didn't. Mom passed the dish with more potatoes and I took another.

'Well,' Mom said, 'it's good to have you here, whatever the reason. I'm just sorry we didn't get the opportunity to have you come stay with us.'

'That would have been a pleasure, Ma'am. But my secretary reserved a room for me at an hotel in Cardigan, so that's where I went. Kind of noisy at night, though. Mrs Takahashi told me she'd met with you last year. She was real impressed by the wildlife around the shore.'

'Well now, why don't you come here anyway?' Mom suggested. 'The guest room is always made up, and it will be good to have you. We can catch up on news of home. Especially since September 11th. I can't tell you how awful it was having to watch that on T.V. and not being able to do a thing about it.'

'Nine-eleven was pretty bad back home, too. Look, if you're serious about me staying here, why, I guess I'd like that. If you really don't mind, that is.'

'We don't mind one bit, do we, David?'

Then I saw my Dad's face. He wasn't delighted

at Mom's suggestion, but he pinned on a smile all the same. 'Like Kate says, Walt, it will be a pleasure to have you. Bring your bags into the office tomorrow, and I'll bring you here tomorrow night after work.'

Whatever Dad was thinking, I thought it would be way cool to have a real Native American living with us. I bet Twm would like to meet him, too. If Walt was into conservation, they'd get on like a house afire!

After dinner the grown-ups talked about Pittsburgh, and the Takahashi Corporation, and all that shop talk got kinda boring, so I went to bed.

'See you tomorrow, Walt!' I said, yawning. Swimming with sharks tires a girl out, dontcha know.

'You sure will. I'll look forward to it. Night, Catrin,' Walt said, waving casually. 'I guess I ought to be getting back to the hotel, too, David. Don't want to keep you folks up too late. Busy day tomorrow.'

Dad drove Walt off to his hotel in our car, and Mom loaded the dishwasher with the dinner things and then followed me upstairs. I heard Dad come back in, and Madoc getting let into the yard for his last-thing-at-night business, and then the front and back doors getting locked. Then Dad came up to bed. Mom must have been still awake, because they started having one of those loud whisper-type arguments parents sometimes have. Mine don't do it often, and I hate it when they do.

'Why d'you have to ask the guy to stay, Katie?' Dad whispered, loud enough for me to hear.

'I hate to hear of someone staying in a hotel when we have a perfectly good guest room here,' she replied. 'Why shouldn't he come stay? Don't you like him?'

'Oh, sure, I like the guy. But right now, honey, I don't know what kind of an agenda he has!' Dad hissed. 'The top guys don't often go visit the subsidiaries unless they're planning to downsize. Maybe he's gonna tell me I'm about to get canned!'

'Oh, that's crazy, David!' Mom hissed back. 'Takahashi won't fire you! Besides, Walt surely wouldn't have agreed to stay here if that was gonna happen, now would he?'

I didn't hear Dad's reply, but it was ages before I got to sleep. Suppose Dad *did* get canned? That would mean we'd all have to go back to Pittsburgh, and I so didn't want to go. Yeah, OK, I know I hadn't wanted to come here in the first place, but that was before I found out how cool Wales is. It's just so different! I even kind of liked the school – at least, the semester I got to go there. I only went for the Autumn and Christmas terms, because right after that Mom and Dad decided to ship me off to La Rochelle to study French, so I got to go to a French *lycée* and that was NOT a whole barrel of laughs, I can tell you. I'll be real glad to get back to Pontpentre-dŵr Comprehensive. I most certainly did not want to go back to my old school in Pittsburgh!

Next morning Mom and Dad were friends again. That's the good thing about my folks, they never stay mad at each other, unlike some of my friends' parents from Pittsburgh. First little spat and they were heading for their lawyers to get themselves a divorce!

I wandered yawning into the kitchen and helped myself to cornflakes, chopped a banana into the dish and poured on milk. Jake was either not awake or off somewhere – he'd gotten himself involved in rugby, which is real big in Wales. They play touch rugby every Saturday morning, and he has ambitions to get on his school team, like Cei.

A pile of books was stacked on the counter, and when I'd finished munching I wandered over and had a look. *How to be a Published Poet* was one of them, and all the others were collections of poems by various people, so I guess Mom's still on the Poetry Enthusiasm. However, there was another book below that one: an old, musty-smelling book with brown spotted pages and paper with uneven edges. The book fell open when I picked it up. It was in real old writing, with f's where 's' should have been, which made it kind of difficult to read until I got the hang of it. It was also in kind of a blobbly black print, and I was about to give up when a couple of familiar words caught my eye.

'*The Legend of the Sea Girl*' it said, (it actually said, '*Fea Girl*', but I translated it) and then the blobby writing carried on down the page.

The Legend of the Sea Girl is told, whereby Owain the Bard, a legendary singer and musician of whom it was said that all things that had song, that he could sing.

I sort of translated that into 'anything that sang, he could imitate'.

The Legend tells how the Bard journeyed to the bottom of the sea to seek counsel from the Sea King himself, so that he could sing the sound of the sea, the one song that eluded him. But when she saw him, the Sea King's Daughter fell in love with him. The bard spurned her, saying that he could not love a woman who wore the tail of a fish. Angry, the Sea King's daughter dragged his boat beneath the waves and drowned him.

The legend tells how the Sea King's Daughter called upon Sea Magic to transform her tail to human legs, and it is said that from that day forward she laboured in a fruitless search for love, believing that somewhere in the Island of the Mighty there would be a man who would love her. The legend describes the exquisite Sea Harp that Owain the Bard had made for the Sea King in return for the Sea's Music, and two other Signs, the Sky Egg and the Earthstone, that are equally mystical. If the Island of the Mighty is to survive, the Sea Girl must keep them, all three, safe. It is written that once she lost them, and the Sixteen Cities of Cantre'r Gwaelod were drowned beneath the waves and all the people with them.

I felt myself turn pale, and a horrible shaky feeling started up inside me. If this legend was true, then the Sea Girl couldn't possibly have all three Signs, because I had the Sky Egg! Why had she given it to me when she knew how important it was to keep them all together? So that meant danger, right?

Mom, carrying a load of bedding for the washing machine, bustled into the kitchen in early morning mode. She's so bright, first thing, that not-good-in-the-morning people, like me, occasionally want to strangle her, no matter how much we happen to love her.

'Morning, honeybun,' she chirped, dropping a kiss on my cheek. 'Sleep well?'

'Mmph,' I said. 'Mom, where did you get this book?'

She peered at it. 'That? Well, it was real weird, sweetheart. I was in Cardigan a week or two ago, and it was market day, and I was kind of idling round picking stuff up, and there in the downstairs part, right in the corner, there was this little whitewashed room just *crammed* with the most interesting stuff! I could have spent a fortune in there, and the old guy running the stall – you should have seen him, Catty, he looked just like an old-time wizard, with white hair and blue eyes and all – well, he said he could tell I was real interested in stuff like that, and he gave me the book as a gift! Isn't that the kindest thing?'

I stared at her. I knew the little old man she was talking about. Hadn't I met him once, in that very room in Cardigan Market the day I found the Sky Egg? The room that, when I went back to look for it, had disappeared. But now, it seemed, it was back – at least temporarily, so that my Mom could lay hands on the book and bring it home for me to find.

'Did the old guy say anything else, Mom?'

She had her head inside the washing machine out in the utility room, and I had to follow her out and repeat myself. She straightened up.

'You know, I think he did! He said not to put the book on a shelf. Books don't belong on shelves, he said, they belong in hands. I think that was kind of cute, don't you? He's right, of course, books do belong in people's hands. I can't abide the kind of folks who buy books by the yard just to make their décor look good!'

'Mmm,' I said, absent-mindedly. 'Mom, can I borrow this to show Twm?'

'Sure, sweetie. Take care of it, though. It's real old, and I'd hate anything to happen to it.'

'Don't worry. I'll take real good care. Mom, do you mind if I head over there today? Or is there anything you'd like me to do first.'

'Well, I do have a lot to do with Walt coming over. Maybe you could dust the guest room for me before you go, see it's tidy, put clean towels and stuff? The bed's made up, so it won't take long.'

'Sure, Mom.' I scooted up the stairs and whizzed around the guest room. I was looking forward to having Walt stay over. I'd never met a Native American before. When I'd done, I whizzed downstairs again, glad I'd helped before rushing off. Now I could go with a clear conscience!

Mom had her recipe book out.

'I'm off now, Mom, OK?'

'Sure, honey. Look, why don't you invite Twm to eat dinner with us tonight? I'm sure he'd like to meet Walt, and I know Walt would be interested in meeting him, too.'

'I will, Mom. Thanks.' I opened the back door to

get my bike from the shed, and a hairy spring boinged at me. I patted Madoc, who licked me comprehensively, his tail wagging with joy.

'Mom, I'll take Madoc with me, get him out of your way and give him some exercise, OK?'

So I left my bike at home and Madoc and I headed for the village – and Twm's cottage.

CHAPTER SEVEN

Madoc bumbled along at the end of the retractable leash, so I could haul him back if a car came, or another dog that looked like it might be a scrapper.

The way to Twm's cottage is long and twisty and overhung with trees and tall hedges. The sun shone through, dappling the roadway, and I ambled along, the book in my backpack, enjoying the peace after La Rochelle's bustle. Madoc came trotting back to check on me, and give my knee a slurp, so I rewound the leash, which was a real lucky thing, because a car suddenly rushed round the bend at us, and if Madoc had been way ahead of me, he might have been hit.

It hurtled past me, long, low, one of those big, black English sort of sneer-on-wheels cars – you know, cars like the Queen of England goes about in. I glanced inside as it slithered past, much too fast for the little country road, and my heart thumped.

Mrs Gwynne-Davies sat like a large, malevolent toad in the back seat, and Miss Critchett was driving, her long red fingernails tapping on the wheel. The two Spoilers we already knew about. Mrs Gwynne-Davies had disappeared from her mansion shortly after we foiled her and her horrible friends last time, and Miss Critchett, who'd been standing in for Dad's secretary, never went back to claim her pay. But now they were both back!

Maybe they didn't see me, because they didn't slow down or stop. I tucked myself back into the shadow of the hedge so that Miss Critchett couldn't see me in her rear-view mirror. As soon as they'd disappeared round the bend in the road, I started to run towards Twm's cottage as fast as my shaky legs would carry me, Madoc barking happily at my sudden (and unusual!) burst of energy.

In the village, out of breath, I slowed to a walk, past the Post Office and down to the cottage. The top half of the stable door was open to the fresh air, so I stuck my head inside and called, 'Anybody home?'

Feet clattered on the wooden stairway in the corner and Twm appeared. 'Oh, it's you, Catrin. Come on in, will you?' He unbolted the other side of the door and held it wide.

I stepped into the darkness, and Madoc jumped up and down against Twm's legs. As he bent to pet him, I said, 'Twm, I've just seen Mrs Gwynne-Davies and Miss Critchett, whizzing along in that big black car.'

Twm straightened up. 'Back, are they? Oh, they couldn't have come back at a worse time.'

'Why?'

'Taid's ill. He woke up this morning with a pain in his chest, and Dr Gethin put him into the Cottage Hospital straight away in case it was his heart. He said he didn't intend to take chances with a man Taid's age.' Twm gave a half-hearted grin. 'If he only knew exactly how old Taid is, he'd have a heart attack himself.'

'Is he all right?'

'I think so. They gave him some pills and stuck a

heart monitor on him, and it seems to be completely normal. So maybe it was something else.'

'You don't suppose –'

'What, the Spoilers? Who knows? We'll have to keep an eye on them, anyway.'

'In the meantime, we're on our own in the hunt for the Sea Girl, right?'

'I suppose we are. Look, I'm going to have a bit of lunch and then go into the hospital to see Taid, see how he is. Do you want to come with me?'

'If you think Taid wouldn't mind. What about Madoc?'

'Oh, we'll shut him up in here, he'll be fine.'

We ate an early lunch of crusty bread and lovely squishy goats' cheese, shut an indignant Madoc up in the kitchen, and then caught a bus into the next town, where the Cottage Hospital was. Taid was sitting up in bed in red, white and green striped pyjamas, very patriotic, and his long, silver beard and hair had sort of exploded in the heat of the ward. He looked like a star with his own personal nimbus! He started grumbling as soon as we reached him.

'*O, Duw,* Twm, what did you let that fool Gethin put me in here for? Nothing wrong with me, nothing at all. Bit of wind, I expect. I'm right as rain, now.'

'Well, good, Taid. But all the same, better safe than sorry,' Twm said, patting the old man's thin arm.

'Safe, is it? If I don't know when nothing's wrong with me, after all the centuries I've been about, I never will. I've forgotten more about medicine than that young lad will ever have time to learn!'

'Don't be such a grouch, Taid. Dr Gethin was only doing what he thought was right.'

'Fair enough. But now I want to go home,' the old man said, scowling.

A nurse appeared beside him. 'Well, dear, how are we feeling now?' she cooed.

'I don't know how you're feeling, *merch fach,*' Taid said firmly, 'but I'm absolutely fine, and I'll thank you to fetch me my trousers so I can go home!'

'Oh, I think Doctor would like you to stay in for at least another night,' the nurse said, 'so you might as well settle down and enjoy your visitors, mightn't you?'

Fairly obviously, nursie was not going to be thwarted, so Taid, grumbling, settled down.

'Taid,' Twm said, 'Catrin's just seen the Spoilers. Mrs Gwynne-Davies and the other one, the one with the fingernails. Critchett.'

'Back, are they?' The old man nodded, a satisfied expression on his face. 'Good. Now we can keep an eye on them. Means the other two won't be long turning up, and then we can see what we're up against.'

That reminded me. I'd been so caught up with seeing the Spoilers and worrying about Taid having a heart attack that I'd forgotten the book. 'Look,' I said, digging for it in my backpack. 'Mom found this in Cardigan Market, in the same place I found the Sky Egg –'

Horror suddenly struck all three of us.

'The Sky Egg!' I gasped. 'Where is it?'

'*O, Arglwydd Dduw!*' Taid groaned. 'I left it on the table beside my bed, in its box. Oh, how could I do such a stupid thing, Twm? Find me my trews, boy, now!'

'No, Taid. You stay here. Catrin and I will go back and make sure the Egg is all right. I'll ring the hospital later, let you know it's safe.'

The bus was ages coming: we had to wait for nearly twenty-five minutes for it, but in our bit of Wales they more or less only run on every other Tuesday when there's an R in the month and it isn't snowing! OK, so I'm exaggerating a bit, but you get the general idea.

At last it grumbled stinkily towards the stop, and we leapt on. I don't think it went more than about ten miles an hour the entire way, but at last it lurched to a halt outside the Post Office in Pontpentre-dŵr and we hurtled off it and ran down the road to the cottage. It was only a matter of yards away, and we could hear Madoc's frantic barking the minute the noisy bus was out of earshot.

'Something's happened!' I gasped, pounding up the front path. 'Madoc isn't in the kitchen any more!'

Twm unlocked the front door and a hysterical Madoc leapt up and down round us like a jack-in-the-box, barking at the top of his lungs. He was getting to be quite a large dog these days; in dog terms he was a teenager, I suppose, and his long legs and muscular body made him a force to be reckoned with. Twm hurtled past him and up the little twisty stairs in the corner of the room. I heard his feet thump across the floorboards, and then his voice yelled, 'It's all right! The Egg's here!'

Relief made my knees wobbly. All the same, something had happened. Madoc calmed slightly and stopped leaping about like a maniac, and I took his floppy ears between my hands and cradled his head. 'Good dog, Madoc! Well d-'

I stopped. Something was caught between his teeth. I prised his jaws apart and wiggled it free. It was a little piece of dark cloth. I started to laugh, and gave him an extra hug.

'Oh, lovely dog! Good dog! You saved the Egg, didn't you?'

Twm reappeared in the doorway. 'What?'

'Madoc had a piece of cloth caught in his teeth. Looks like he bit someone, Twm! Someone must have gotten inside and Twm saw them off.' I handed the cloth over to him.

His face was grim. 'You'd better not let the Egg out of your sight, Catrin. It looks like things are beginning to happen, fast!' He handed me the box and I opened it. Waves of cold came off it, and I shivered. I closed the box and tucked it into my backpack.

'Now we know the Egg is safe,' Twm said, 'what were you telling Taid about a book?'

'Oh, yeah!' I dug the book out of the front pocket of the backpack. 'Mom got this, and when I picked it up, it fell open at the legend of the Sea Girl – real weird stuff about a Bard. She didn't always have legs, Twm, once she had a tail, but she kind of magicked it away somehow, so she could go on land when she wanted.'

Twm read the story, frowning at the old-fashioned print. 'I know this story,' he said, 'My Mam told it to me ages ago, but –' he turned over to the next page – 'there's a bit here she didn't tell me. Look.' He handed the book over, and I read on.

The legend warns that should the Sea Girl succeed in leaving her underwater home, then the Signs have been parted. The three Signs are all that keep her in the Sea King's realm, and if one should be lost, then for the sake of the Island of the Mighty, they must be reunited.

If Dark Ones are in the ascendant, it is written that the Island of the Mighty will fall. First, its seas will be poisoned, and then the land, the sky, and all that the Great One has created. The Signs cannot be reunited by magic, but the power of the Earth, the Sky and the Sea must if necessary be invoked to recover them. In times of great peril the bearer of the Sign and the pursuer of the Quest will be helped by an Ancient One from the land that was Cymru-claimed. Only when the secrets of the Dark Ones are uncovered will the Sea Girl return to her father's realm and the Island of the Mighty be saved.

'What's the Island of the Mighty, Twm?'

'The Old Name for Britain. Once, all of Britain – Brython, as it was then, was Celtic and spoke Welsh – you know, think of the Mabinogion stories. In those it is called the Island of the Mighty. But what I think it means now is just Wales. Or maybe just the Celtic nations, I don't know for sure. Whatever. We have to solve the riddles!'

'Sure we do, Twm. Just one problem. We don't know what the secrets are, or even how to find out!'

'Maybe Taid will know something. And if he doesn't, I'll ask my Mam.'

'Oh, I forgot. Mom and Dad have asked you to dinner tonight. Can you come? There's someone we'd really like you to meet.'

'I don't know, Catrin. There's Cei to worry about. He's off playing Dragon rugby with Jake. He should be home soon.' He looked at his watch. 'In fact, he's late. Come on, let's go down to the rugby club and fetch him.'

Just as we were about to leave, however, the door burst open and our two brothers erupted into the little room, followed by a third boy, who hung about nervously in the doorway.

'Oh, great, Catty, you're here. Can you tell Mom that Cei and me are going to stay with Rhodri tonight? Rhodri's Mom will bring us back tomorrow.'

'Better plan, Jake,' I fished in my pocket and threw him a twenty pence piece for the call-box. 'Phone home, E.T. If she says you can stay, great.'

She did, of course. My Mom never says no if she can say yes, and she only says no if there's a real good reason. Besides, she knows Rhodri's Mom and Dad, and likes them.

So, the Egg safely stowed in my backpack, Twm and I locked up the little house and set off to eat dinner at my house.

CHAPTER EIGHT

The house was filled with good smells – roasting chicken and my all-time favourite, chocolate brownies, which meant brownies and ice-cream for dessert. Yum. Twm was sniffing like a bloodhound.

'Hi, Twm,' Mom said, 'good to see you again. How's Taid?'

'He's in hospital, Mrs Morgan,' Twm mumbled through the warm brownie she'd handed him. 'Doctor thought perhaps his heart, but that's fine, thank goodness. Hope he'll be home tomorrow.'

'Oh, my goodness!' Mom turned from her cooking to frown at him. 'Well, don't let him overdo it. You can't be too careful with an old gentleman like Taid.'

'I could roll him in bubblewrap and cottonwool and pack him in a tea-chest, Mrs Morgan, but I still couldn't be careful with him. Taid does what he wants, when he wants, I'm afraid.'

Mom laughed. 'I guess so. All the same, if we can help –'

'I'll be sure to ask,' Twm said, finishing the brownie.

'Cat, honey, would you set the table, please?' Mom asked, tossing me a tablecloth. 'Dad and Walt will be home soon, and we'll eat as soon as Walt's settled in and they've washed up.'

Twm stayed in the kitchen chatting to Mom, who

gave him the potatoes to bash and butter, and I set the table at a gallop, not wanting to miss any of the conversation. When I got back in the kitchen, however, Mom was in full flight on her latest Enthusiasm, and Twm's eyes were looking kind of glazed.

'I used to turn my nose up at handicrafts, Twm,' she was saying, putting the golden-brown chicken on its carving dish in the warming oven, 'but I went to just one bear-making class and I was hooked! I could just sit for hours stitching my bears! I'm thinking of asking the gift shop in Cardigan if they'll sell them for me. I try to make each one different, and they are so *cute*! I'll show you after dinner.'

Behind her back I was making frantic 'NO!!!' signals at him, but he's such a creep around my Mom.

'I'd love to see them, Mrs Morgan,' he said. 'I'm sure they're beautiful. Do you make them from fur or cloth? Glass eyes or embroidered?'

I mouthed, 'rat fink!' at him, and he pulled a face back. We'd be stuck for hours looking at the bears, now. She'd made dozens, and her workroom was starting to overflow into all the bedrooms. It wouldn't be long before 'Katie's Booful Bears' took over the world! I sure hoped the gift shop *would* sell them – we could get rid of some then!

Then Dad's key scraped into the lock and he and Walt came in. Walt was wearing a formal suit, and it looked kinda weird with his braids, I can tell you! I deliberately hadn't told Twm anything about him being Native American, or anything else, and I quite enjoyed the way astonishment made him miss a step when we went into the living room to greet them.

'Twm, boy!' Dad smiled, sticking out his hand to shake. 'Good to see you again. We missed you when Catty went to France. You shouldn't be a stranger, you should come by whenever you want.'

Missed him, did they? How do they think *I* felt, then?

'Thanks, Mr Morgan. I'll remember that.'

'You won't have to,' I said grimly. 'They're not sending me anywhere else, ever.'

'Walt,' Dad went on, turning to introduce him, 'this is Catty's friend, Twm. Twm, this is Walter He-Who-Flies-With-Eagles.'

Twm put out his hand and Walt took it. It was a bit as if time had stopped, suddenly, because they held the handshake for what seemed like an age. Twm and Walt looked deep into each other's eyes, as if they were recognising old friends, and then stepped apart.

'G-good to meet you, sir,' Twm stammered.

He was off-balance, somehow, and I wondered why.

'Walt,' the big man said. 'Call me Walt. Tell me, Twm. Did you ever meet Mrs Takahashi?'

A grin spread across Twm's face. 'Oh, yes, indeed I did. Oh, yes.'

Walt grinned back. 'That explains a whole lot.'

Like, pardon? I looked from one to the other, totally mystified. This was, like, majorly, majorly weird.

Dad took Walt upstairs to unpack, shower and

change, and we all sat down to dinner when they came down. Dad carved (he likes to do that: I think he pretends he's a brain surgeon or something!) and Mom passed the vegetables and gravy. I was so hungry all I could think about was food for a while, and then I picked up on a conversation.

'My Dad is Iroquois,' Walt was telling Twm, 'but my Mom's ancestors were from a different tribe, one that's sadly died out now. That happened to a lot of the smaller tribes.'

I knew about that. Not much Native American history was taught in US schools, but I'd read books about it. When the white man arrived in America he took the land but brought the white man's diseases, and guns, and whisky, and none of those encourages a long life! It's always seemed real weird to me, the fuss folks made a while ago celebrating the Bicentennial. Like, two hundred years? Some big deal when the Native Americans had been around for thousands of years!

When the chicken was gone, we got into the brownies and ice cream in a big way. My Mom discovered these totally amazing ice-creams in Wales: it isn't like Ben and Jerry's, but it's equally gorgeous – living in Ceredigion, half way down Wales, we get Cadwallader's ice-cream from the north, and Thayer's from the south. Both really yummy.

By this time Twm and Walt were deep into discussing the environment: turns out Walt's a founder member of Greenpeace America, and as hot on the subject as Twm is. They talked about whaling, and the ozone layer, and global warming, then got on to red kites and wind farms, stuff like that, until my eyes started to cross with boredom. Not that I'm not interested in conservation, but hey, it had been a long day.

Towards the end of the evening, Dad opened the door in the kitchen that led to the outhouse. Madoc hurtled past him and into the sitting room, skidding on the rag rug and ending in a heap at Walt's feet. He'd been shut up the whole time Walt had been here last evening, so Walt hadn't met the hairy monster yet.

Madoc recovered his dignity and trotted over to Walt, sniffed his ankles and when Walt extended his hand to him, sniffed that too, and gave it a tentative lick. Then he sat at his feet while Walt scratched his chest in exactly the place he liked to be scratched best.

'Hello, little brother,' Walt rumbled in his deep voice, 'what do they call you?'

'Madoc,' I said, and was a bit bemused when Walt began to laugh.

'Now that's some coincidence!' he chuckled. 'Well, hi, Madoc!'

'Coincidence?' Mom said, puzzled, 'why coincidence?'

Twm sat up straight in his chair. 'I think I know,' he said, his eyes glittering with excitement. 'Your Mother's tribe – the one that died out – it was the Mandan tribe, wasn't it?'

Walt glanced at him. 'Well now. You know more of

our history than most Americans. You got it. I'm part Mandan.'

Twm looked at me. I couldn't quite read his expression. It was sort of triumph, but there was something else. What was it? Relief?

I shrugged, signifying that I wasn't getting the message, but Twm was speaking again.

'So, Walt, there's a possibility that you're part Welsh, too?'

'A big possibility,' Walt confirmed. 'I guess you know the story, right?'

'Story?' Mom said, 'what story?'

'Can't you remember why we named the dog Madoc?' Dad said suddenly. 'It was because he was so fascinated by the sea when he was a pup. Madoc was a Welsh sailor prince. Legend said he discovered America somehow, but I guess that's all it is, a nice old legend.'

Walt was shaking his head. 'With respect, David, you're wrong. My people have their own legends about a great canoe with a dragon head that came from far away, carrying fair-skinned people. They brought us bull-boats – the Welsh call them coracles – to use when we fished, and they brought their language. There's a ton of evidence – physical as well as our legends – that a Welshman called Madoc discovered America in 1170, long before Columbus got to us in 1492. The D.A.R. – that's the Daughters of the American Revolution, Twm – even erected a plaque on the beach at Mobile, Alabama, where Madoc was supposed to have landed, and the D.A.R.

are never wrong! So yeah, I'm part Welsh, I guess. A small part, but it's certainly there.'

Twm was just about bursting with excitement. Then suddenly, I realised why. I remembered the legend in the book Mom had found . . .

In times of great peril the bearer of the Sign and the pursuer of the Quest will be helped by an Ancient One from a land that was Cymru-claimed . . .

Cymru is what the Welsh call Wales, right? So if Madoc got there in 1170, and claimed it for Wales, that means America had been *Cymru-claimed*! Oh, wow! I stared at Walt with new eyes. Maybe he was our helper! Maybe that explained why Mrs Takahashi had sent him. Had she somehow known we needed help? Nah. Not possible. Was it?

I glanced at Twm. His eyes were sparkling. He stared solemnly at me and nodded. He knew what I was thinking, because he was way ahead of me. All the same, he wasn't jumping in and asking – not in front of Mom and Dad, anyway!

It was right then that the telephone rang. Dad got up to answer it, and Mom disappeared into the kitchen to make more coffee. Walt rubbed Madoc's head and looked into his eyes.

'This is a special dog, Catrin,' he said. 'Dogs with these light eyes see a whole lot more than most dogs.'

'I know,' I said, remembering what Dad had said when we got the pup. 'Old Welsh farmers call dogs with eyes like Madoc's "dogs that have seen the wind". Madoc's special anyway, Walt. And he certainly knows who he likes!' Madoc was trying to insinuate himself onto the chair beside Walt. 'You'll never get rid of him now.'

Dad turned from the telephone. 'Twm,' he called, 'it's for you. Don't worry, it's not the hospital. It's Cei.'

'Cei? What does he want?'

'Only one way to find out!' Dad passed the phone to him.

'Cei? What is it? Are you all right?'

I couldn't hear Cei's answer, of course, but I could tell from Twm's expression there was something wrong.

'Where?' he said urgently. 'Which end? Just the one? Right. Stay close to it. Don't let anyone else near it. I'm coming now.'

Walt and Dad were staring at him and I was on my feet. 'What's the matter?'

'Cei, Jake and Rhodri are having a beach barbecue with Rhodri's Mam and Dad. They've found a dolphin, stranded. Cei says it's still alive. I've got to go and see what I can do.'

'I'll come with you,' I said.

'And me,' Dad said. 'I'll get a torch.'

'I'm coming too,' Walt was on his feet and heading for the door.

'Doesn't anyone want coffee?' Mom appeared from the kitchen with a tray.

'Later, Mom, thanks!' I called, following the others out of the front door and into the darkness.

CHAPTER NINE

We climbed into Dad's car and headed for Tresaith, from where Cei had telephoned. The car twisted through the dark lanes, then through the little village and down to the steep hill to the shore. Rhodri's Mom was standing at the top of the beach near the lifebelt stand, and a fire burned halfway down the beach, lighting up the pebbly sand with an eerie, flickering glow.

'Where is it?' Twm asked, not bothering with "hello" and "how are you". However, Rhodri's Mom obviously knew Twm well enough to know that politeness wasn't his style when his beloved creatures were at risk, and just led the way. We stumbled and scrambled across the pebbles to the cliffs over to the right, near where a small waterfall plunged from the heights to splatter on the beach. Jake, Rhodri, his Dad and Cei were crouched beside a dark, motionless hump on the sand. Apart from the sea hissing on the sand, the night was silent except for a weird, conversational whistling that I suddenly realised was the dolphin. Only that and the convulsive movement of its blowhole opening and closing showed that it was still alive.

Twm and I knelt beside the creature, and Twm ran his hand over its back. Walt took the torch from Dad and shone it along the dolphin's body.

'He isn't hurt, as far as I can tell,' Twm whispered, still stroking the long grey body reassuringly. The moon chose that minute to emerge from a bank of clouds, and the long bottlenosed shape took on a silvery gleam. 'He needs to be kept wet. What can we carry seawater in?'

'There's a picnic cooler,' Rhodri's Mom offered. 'I'll go and get it.'

She ran up the beach to the fire, and I saw her upend the cooler onto a blanket, canned drinks, plastic sandwich boxes, all the paraphernalia of a beach picnic all tumbled haphazardly down. Cei, thinking fast, tied a knot in the neck of his waterproof jacket and filled that, Walt, Jake, my Dad and Rhodri's, did the same, and they made a chain to the incoming tide, pouring gallon after gallon of water on the barely moving body.

Twm was lying alongside the dolphin, his head pressed to the bulge above the beaked nose, imitating the dolphin's squeaks and whistles. It was several minutes before I realised that the dolphin was *listening* and *answering*. What else did I expect? This was Twm, right?

Load after load of cold seawater poured over the dolphin and Twm, and still he didn't move. When Rhodri's Mom, Cei and Jake had gotten tired and too slow at the seawater run, Rhodri and I took over, and joined Walt in the water carrying. Walt seemed tireless. The tide crept closer and closer, but seemed to be coming so slowly that by the time it was lapping at the dolphin's outstretched tail, I was so tired, wet and cold I could hardly stand up. We watched the rippling waves inch up the dolphin's body, along the slender, powerful tail, over the dorsal fin, over the rounded head until it lapped the edge of the blowhole.

'Right, now,' Twm said, scrambling to his feet, drenched to the skin, 'roll him over. Help me! *Dere 'mlaen, boi bach!* Come on, lovely boy!'

The dolphin was smooth and icy cold under my hands as I tugged and shoved and heaved. We got him right way up, and waited, supporting him on each side while the tide washed in, deeper and deeper. Cei, Jake and Rhodri had forgotten they were tough and grown-up, and were clutching each other, desperate to see that lithe body launched safely into its natural habitat.

At last the water was deep enough. The dolphin twitched its tail and was floating. With Twm on one side, Walt on the other, they walked out into the waves with it, guiding it, gently pushing it, encouraging it to go. When they were waist-deep they released it. I twisted my hands together and prayed that it wouldn't immediately beach itself again – sometimes they do that, because their radar has been messed up somehow. But the dolphin circled them once, nudged Twm with his nose, and then we saw the curve of his back disappear beneath the waves, the dorsal fin jutting, heading out, far out, to sea.

The three boys danced like dervishes beside me on the beach, crying and laughing and slapping each other's backs, all at the same time. Rhodri's Mom was crying too, and my Dad and Rhodri's were shaking hands and grinning. Twm and Walt, soaked to the skin and shivering with cold, waded ashore, glancing behind them every so often to make sure the dark shape was still heading out to sea.

Walt, too, was smiling, happiness spread across the high-cheekboned face, white teeth gleaming in the darkness, but Twm – Twm's face, when Dad shone the torch on him, was white and grim.

'What's the m –' I began, but he shook his head, silencing me.

We climbed back into Dad's car, and Cei, Rhodri and his parents into theirs, and we set off for our separate homes.

Twm and I sat in the back-seat, and Walt sat beside Dad up front. The car heater kicked in and gradually warm air began to circulate. Twm's hair dripped salt, and he was so wet that nothing would warm him. I looked at him, but he didn't speak; all he did was reach for my hand and hold it, tight. I hoped my Dad couldn't see, or I'd be on the next flight back to La Rochelle!

Back at the Toll House, Mom chased Twm and Walt up the stairs, Walt into the shower, Twm into a hot bath, and Dad hunted up spare clothes for Twm. When he came downstairs again Mom had hot drinks and sandwiches ready for all of us, and despite the huge meal we'd eaten earlier, we were more than ready for them.

'Twm, there's no one at your cottage tonight, so you'll stay here,' Mom decided. 'You can sleep in Jake's bed.'

Twm, ever independent, opened his mouth to

protest, but it turned into a huge yawn. He gave in, grinned, and said, 'Thanks, Mrs Morgan. I'm too tired to go anywhere, to be honest with you.'

Walt caught Twm's yawn too. 'Oh, excuse me! I guess I'll hit the sack, Kate, if you guys don't mind. The last thing I was expecting to do tonight was take a swim after dinner!'

Mom and Dad went up shortly afterwards, and Twm and I were left alone in the living room. Dad turned in the doorway and glanced back, looking from one of us to the other.

'Not too late, you two,' he said gruffly. 'I guess Twm will want to be at the hospital early.'

I rolled my eyes. 'Sure, Dad,' I said, seeing right through his bluff. What he meant was, 'I'm going to bed and I'm not real happy about leaving you two alone down here.'

What did he think we were gonna do? Neck? For Pete's sake! All the same, when Twm took my hand again, I didn't pull away.

'Right, give!' I ordered. 'What happened? Why did the dolphin beach itself? And don't pretend you don't know, Twm, because I heard you talk to it.'

'He was in a bad way, Catrin,' he said slowly, 'and I couldn't understand a lot of what he said. He seemed sort of confused. He said that his Clan was out in the Bay, when they heard their Seanames being called. So of course, they went.'

'Seanames?'

'Seanames. Dolphins have secret names, Seanames, that only they know.'

'I know they communicate, those whistles and clicks and squeaks and stuff, but I didn't know they had names.'

'The clicks are their way of echo-location, like bats, squeaking. The way they talk is the whistle and squeak. And of course they have names. How would they call to each other if they didn't?'

Somehow it had never occurred to me that dolphins had names. That took a minute or two to sink in. 'So some other dolphins were calling their Seanames, right? And the big guy got himself lost and ended up beached?'

Twm shook his head. 'Wish it had been. It's much worse than that. What happened was that dolphin, the one that leads the Clan, heard someone call his name, and if dolphins hear their Seanames, they'll follow the call. Luckily, he swam faster than the others, and he reached the end of the sea first. He'd already beached himself before he realised he was being tricked, and it was too late for him to save himself. Once he was on the sand, he couldn't get back into the sea. He tried, but his strength gave out. He'd swum a long way and was tired. He used his last energy to call a warning to the others to keep away. Luckily, they obeyed, or all of them would have been stranded, and most of them would probably have died. We were lucky that the Seaname callers didn't know that Cei and his friends would be on the beach tonight. He'd have died, Catrin'

I shivered at the thought of the beautiful creature dying alone on a dark beach. 'Thank goodness for beach barbecues! But Twm, if it wasn't a dolphin that called him, then what was it?'

'Can't you guess? The Spoilers, of course.'

I stared at him. 'I know they're the bad guys, but why would they want to do that? Kill the dolphins, I mean?'

Twm shrugged. 'Who knows? But trust me, Catrin, they'll have a reason. It's up to us to find out what it is.'

'Do you suppose that this is the first secret?'

'Could be. I mean, we can take it as read that the secrets are going to be something we are going to have to uncover – and then stop whatever bad things they're planning from happening, like last time.'

'And once again, we only have one of the Sea-Girl's Signs to help us.' I sighed. 'And not a solitary clue about where to look for the Sea Girl to find the other two. It's, like, totally, majorly impossible.'

Twm looked determined. 'Nothing's impossible. At least now we know that the Spoilers are targeting the sea-creatures, don't we? That's a start. Anyway, we haven't asked my Mam, yet. She should be able to help. And once Taid is out of hospital, perhaps he can help us somehow. Don't worry, Catrin, we'll do it. We've got to, haven't we? It's up to us.' He put his arm around my shoulders, and I was so worried I hardly noticed.

'All the same,' I muttered, unconsciously snuggling in, 'I wish we at least knew who the other two Spoilers were. That would be a start, wouldn't it?' A terrible thought struck me. 'Twm, you don't suppose – oh, one of them couldn't be Walt, could it?'

'Not a chance. Remember when we shook hands tonight – blimey, was it only tonight? – well, touching him was like getting an electric shock. It was the same for him, too, I could tell by his face. No, he's a Keeper, like us. Didn't you see the way he was working with the dolphin? A Spoiler couldn't do that.'

'Couldn't, or wouldn't?'

'Couldn't. I'm sure that if a Spoiler touched a living creature, the creature would recognise it. Even if it didn't turn on the Spoiler, it would have an effect on it. The dolphin would have died tonight, even if the Spoiler had been pretending to help by pouring seawater over it. That's one thing that's good. They can't get close to us by pretending to be something they're not. Something inside us will always warn us.'

About that time, I suddenly realised how good his arm felt, wrapped round me like that, and I could feel his chest rising and falling against me. I turned my head to look up at him, and he looked down and me, and I swear we might have –

'Catty? Twm? Time you guys were in bed!'

My Dad's voice broke the spell. We shot apart like frightened bunnies.

'Night, Twm,' I mumbled, my face bright red.

'Night, Catrin,' he replied, equally pink.

Honestly, fathers!

CHAPTER TEN

Next morning, at breakfast, Dad gave me a Stern Look. The sort of look that says 'whatever you guys were up to last night, I don't approve, because you're my daughter and you're still a little girl.' Except I'm not, not any more. I'm also the Sea Girl, and although Dad doesn't know that, I know it, and I know that I have to do stuff that he most definitely wouldn't approve of. But like the guy said, a man's gotta do what a man's gotta do, and so's a gal, right?

It was Saturday, but all the same, Dad and Walt were going into the factory to look at some stuff. Mom was locked away in her studio Bear-making, Jake was still with Cei and Rhodri – Twm was going to stay with us until Taid was out of hospital – so we were headed for the hospital to see how Taid was doing. I put the Sky Egg safely in my backpack. No way was I gonna leave it around for a Spoiler to steal.

The bus rattled and grumbled into the town, and by the time we'd gotten off I felt real sick from the diesel fumes and the twisty-turny lanes. Once the fresh air hit, I felt better, but all the same I had this weird feeling that something was about to happen. I found myself looking over my shoulder the whole time, you know the feeling?

Taid was sitting in a high-backed chair beside his

bed, which had its sheets so tightly tucked in that he'd need a crowbar to get back into it!

Twm bent and kissed the old man's cheek, and Taid scowled at him.

'I'm fed up with this place, boy. I want to go home,' he grumbled.

'I know, Taid. Look, you talk to Catrin, I'll go and ask the ward sister if you can go.' Taid glowered at his grandson's departing back. 'I don't much care what that old sister says, Catrin *cariad*. Not staying here another night, I'm not. Nothing wrong with me. Fit as a flea, I am.'

I patted his hand. 'I know, Taid. Maybe we can take you home right now. We could get a cab, you'd be home in no time at all.'

'Cab?' Taid's eyebrows shot up into his white fluff of hair. 'A *taxi-cab*? Goodness me, whatever for? No, we'll catch the bus.'

I doubted Twm would let him, but I didn't say a word.

The old man leaned over conspiratorially. 'Truth is, Catrin, I've got to get out of here. Not some whim, no, not at all. Something in this place is bothering me, and I can't tell what.'

Twm came back then, before I had time to ask questions. From his face I could tell that the news was bad.

'Sorry, Taid,' he said. 'Sister says you can't come out yet. According to your notes, the scan the doctors did wasn't at all clear for some reason, so they're going to do it again.'

I wasn't surprised the scan didn't work. The last thing Taid wanted was his magical innards exposed!

Taid stood up. 'No! I'm not staying here a minute longer. I'll sign myself out. Get me the form. I'm going home. This place is full of old people. Twm, boy, I've got to go home!'

Old? I mean, he counted his own age in centuries! The old guys in here were babies compared to him.

Twm sat on the bed. 'Oh, Taid, please stay. If you come home now, and something happens to you, what will Cei and I do? We can't do without you, Taid, you know that.'

'Managing all right without me at the moment, aren't you?' he grumbled, but he sat in his chair again.

'Only because Cei is staying with Rhodri's parents. But he can't stay there forever, can he?'

The old man's bright blue eyes were almost hidden by scowling eyebrows. 'All right. I'll stay. But like it or not, Friday I'm coming out of here. Not going to be here next Friday, that I'm not, so like it or lump it I'll be home.'

'All right, Taid. I know all about Friday. But don't get yourself all worked up, all right? You won't get well if you're all upset. So calm down and concentrate on getting better.'

'Rubbish!' Taid muttered. 'You're talking rubbish, boy! "Concentrate on getting better" indeed. Humph!'

All the same, by the time we left, he was sitting up straight and watching the progress of the lunch trolley around the ward.

'What's so special about Friday?' I asked idly, as we made our way to the bus stop.

'Anniversary of the night Mam went,' Twm said shortly. 'We like to be together that night.'

'What do you mean, "Mam went"?' I asked. 'Where did she go?'

He was silent for a while. Then, he flashed a quick glance at me, as if checking to make sure I really wanted to know, or maybe that I was a safe person to tell.

'Mam didn't go anywhere, really. She's still here. Only we can't see her, that's all.'

I stared at him. 'What, like a ghost or something?'

'No, *twpsyn*! No such thing as ghosts, is there! I'm surprised you haven't guessed. My Mam is Nimue, isn't she!'

'Nimue?' I tripped over my own feet I was so startled. 'You mean, like, *the* Nimue?'

'There is only one Nimue, Catrin.'

'The Nimue that locked Merlin up in an oak tree for a couple of centuries? That Nimue?'

'That's the one.'

'Then who's your fa – oh, no, Twm. You're winding me up, right?'

He shook his head and kicked a stone. It ricocheted off a wall and earned him a scowl from an old lady. 'No, I wouldn't do that. 'S true.'

'You're telling me that your *Mom* is Nimue?'

'And Taid isn't my Taid. He's Merlin.'

'What? Oh, come on! You're saying he's actually *Merlin*? Like, *the* Merlin?'

102

He nodded. 'The one and only.'

'So how come he's here and your Mom isn't?'

'It's a long story. Mam shut Merlin up in an oak tree for a whole load of reasons. One was because he did some stupid things, the other was for his own safety. There came a time when necromancers weren't the most popular people around: some people took against witches and wizards, and used to do nasty things to them.'

'How could they, if they were magic? Couldn't they just vanish themselves?'

'They could – except you remember what we did with the Earthstone? Where we had to put it?'

'In an iron box, because magic can't pass through – oh, I get it. You're saying they locked them up in iron boxes or something?'

He nodded. 'Forever. So they died. Came a time when there weren't many Old Ones left, and even fewer of the People of the Light. There were only the Darksiders – the Spoilers, and they were usually behind the witch-hunters. When Mam thought it was safe again, then she let Merlin out of his tree.'

I felt a bit out of my tree myself. My head was whirling, trying to take it all in. 'So, where's your Mom, and why did she go there?'

'She's gone back to her people on the Lightside. She made a bargain, see. She could give birth to the next generation, but once she had done that, she couldn't stay earthbound any longer. But she's still here, all the same. You just have to know where to look for her.'

'So you and Cei – you're the next generation?'

'Mmm. Only Cei doesn't know the history of it yet. He's too young. Taid will tell him when he's old enough to understand.'

'So where does he think your Mom's gone?'

Twm shrugged. 'Don't know. I think he's got an idea – but he hasn't asked. When he asks, then he'll be old enough to know. He was only a tiny baby when she went. Doesn't really remember her.'

We walked in silence for a while. I was still trying to take in what Twm had told me. Then, suddenly, I remembered something Taid had said. 'Twm, while you were talking to the ward sister, Taid said that he didn't want to stay in hospital any longer because there was something in there that was bothering him. He couldn't tell what it was, but he was worried about it. But maybe he's just old and doesn't like the helpless feeling being in hospital gives him.'

'Helpless? Taid's never helpless. He could be out of there in a second if he wanted to, and the nurses would forget he'd ever been there.'

'Then why doesn't he?'

'Because he's ill, Catrin. He's so old, I think he knows he's just beginning to wind down, like an old clock. He's tired of living, and he's tired of looking after Cei and me, and he's tired of being without Mam. But he has to stay here until we're old enough to be independent. So when he gets aches and pains, he gets treatment for them. But as soon as Cei is old enough, or I'm old enough to take care of Cei, he'll be gone.'

104

'Oh, Twm! Then you'll be all alone, won't you?'

He stopped short and looked at me. 'Alone? Of course not. Like I told you, they'll still be there, around us, won't they? Nimue and Merlin. Still there. And there's the creatures, and there's you. I'll never be alone.'

I stared at him in consternation. 'But in a year or two, my family is going back to the US, Twm! I thought you knew that! Mom and Dad won't go back without me.'

He shook his head. 'Wait and see, Catrin. You'll never leave Wales forever, none of you. Your life – and theirs – is here. I've seen it written. That's the thing about Wales. Gets under your skin, into your bones and your blood, and there's nothing you can do about it. You may go back for a while, but Wales will call you, and you'll come back. Oh, you'll come back.'

'Written? What do you mean, written?'

'It's in the legends, Catrin.'

Well, what did I know?

When the bus rattled to a halt about a mile away from the Toll House, we dawdled back up the lane, both of us lost in our own thoughts. I liked the idea of staying here. He was right: Wales was in my blood, now. The States was just a distant memory. Didn't seem real any more.

Mom was waiting at the garden gate. 'Twm, Catrin, thank heaven you guys are back! The hospital telephoned. You need to get back there, real quick. Taid's taken a turn for the worse!'

Twm's face went white.

'But we've only just left him!' I stammered. 'He was fine when we left!'

'Well, it seems he isn't fine now,' Mom said. 'Jump in the car, both of you. I'll drive you. Hurry!'

In the backseat, Twm's hand crept into mine. *Taid, I willed him, Taid, you can't die. You're Merlin! Merlin is forever!*

CHAPTER ELEVEN

Mom dropped Twm at the front door of the hospital while she found a parking space, then she and I sprinted across the parking lot and in through the swing doors, my backpack with the freezing Sky Egg thumping on my back. Twm led the way upstairs and into Taid's ward. The drapes were drawn round his bed, and neither Mom nor I felt we could peek inside. Whatever was going on was private between Twm and the medical staff.

After a couple of minutes of watching people's behinds bulge the flowery fabric, and listening to hushed, concerned voices coming from inside, I turned away, too anxious to look any more, and glanced down the ward.

Out of the corner of my eye I saw someone walk past the open door of the ward. My brain registered 'DANGER' but when I looked back, the person was gone. So who had it been?

'Mom,' I whispered, the way you do in hospitals, 'you stay here. Tell Twm I'll be back. I – I – um – need to find the bathroom.'

I shot out through the swing doors and into the corridor. It stretched in both directions, empty of people. There were odd gurneys standing about, and doors with portholes in them, and the sound of voices. So what had gotten my attention?

I tiptoed down the corridor, first in one direction, then in the other, peering into all the rooms, looking for the thing that had alerted me. Patients in small side wards chatted to visitors or slept with their mouths agape. Nurses' station, unmanned; ward kitchens, sluice room, treatment room, patients' bathrooms. And then, at the end of the corridor, I noticed another door. The window in it was frosted glass, no way of seeing who was inside. But on the door was a typewritten card enclosed in one of those square metal frames.

MS MORDREDA CRITCHETT
WARD SECRETARY

The sound of a computer printer filtered through the closed door. A Spoiler, and in the hospital! I backed away, nervously, as if she could sense me through the wood. Even if Taid hadn't seen her, he had known she was there. No wonder he'd taken a turn for the worse! How could we leave him in hospital, with her so close and able to get at him whenever she felt like it? We had to get him out. Anger bubbled up in me. How dare she? A helpless old man! Whatever she'd done to him, she'd pay, somehow.

I dashed back to the ward. The drapes were drawn back from around the bed and the doctors and nurses were talking to Mom at the end of the ward, all of them looking serious. Taid lay flat on his back in the bed, his nose yellow and beak-like against the white hospital pillows.

Twm beckoned me closer. 'He's all right,' he whispered. 'He had pains in his chest again, but they still say there's nothing wrong with his heart.'

A dry old voice rustled from the pillows. 'Of course it isn't my heart. Heart's fine, boy! It's this place. I've got to get out of here. You've got to get me out, Twm!'

'But why, Taid? Everyone's trying to make you better! You're safe in here!'

The old man shook his head feebly on the pillows, his blue eyes fixed on Twm's face.

'He isn't, Twm!' I whispered. 'He isn't safe at all. There's a Spoiler here. The Critchett woman. She's in the office, working.'

Taid clutched my hand. 'I knew it! Said there was something, didn't I, *cariad*? Now will you listen to me, Twm? Get me out!'

'But you're ill, Taid. How can I talk them into letting you come home when you're worse than you were when you came in?'

'And why do you think that is, Twm? Because there's a Spoiler getting at me, that's why. If I stay in here any longer I might never come out! She could change my notes, make them give me iron tablets – or worse!'

'He's right, Twm. We've got to spring him somehow,' I urged.

'But how can we? The doctor has sent for a specialist from Bronglais! They won't *let* me take him out!'

'Then we'll come steal him!' I said fiercely. 'Either

109

that or we refuse to leave his side. We have to protect him from the Spoiler, Twm!'

Twm shoved his fingers into his hair and moaned. 'What, break into the hospital? How are we going to do that, with security people all over the place? And there's the nurses. They aren't going to stand for us pinching one of their patients.'

An idea hit me. 'I know! Taid – do you have any of your fairy dust left?'

'Fairy dust?' The old man looked puzzled for an instant, then his lips parted in a weak grin. 'Of course I have! In the cupboard, Twm! *Duw, fachgen!* Has your brain taken a holiday?'

Twm looked at me, hope on his face. 'Of course! The magic powder! Look, Taid. Hang on. We'll be back as soon as we can. And if that woman comes close, scream blue murder, right? Pretend you're having a fit or something.'

'No need to pretend, boy. If she comes close, I'll have a spectacular one, no problem there!'

He still looked ill when we left him, but at least he was looking less worried.

We got Mom to stop by Twm's cottage on the way home on the pretext of picking up some clean pyjamas for Taid. Twm opened the cupboard and took out a couple of packets of the silvery brown powder. He gave half to me, and slipped the rest into his own pocket. I put my supply into the backpack, next to the Sky Egg. The cold from the Egg was coming through the box, and there were ice crystals on the outside of it, now.

Dad and Walt weren't back – Dad had stopped by the Pugh's pub in Aberaeron to introduce him to Mr and Mrs P. They'd be real interested to meet a part-Welsh Native American! They probably wouldn't get away from there until Thanksgiving, if they were lucky, not when the guys in the bar got to hear about it!

But they finally got home, and we ate dinner, and then Twm and I said we were going out for a walk. We took a torch and said not to worry – we were going to maybe walk into the village, have a word with Rhodri's Mom and Dad, update them on how Taid was doing. Mom and Dad accepted that, no worries, and we'd only said 'maybe', so we hadn't *exactly* lied, had we?

We caught the last bus to town and the cottage hospital. We'd take a cab back once we'd rescued Taid. It felt like a commando raid, slithering through the doors and into the little foyer. We spent a whole lot of time hiding behind doors while folks went past, and ducking in and out of rooms, but eventually we managed to reach the ward where Taid was, without being spotted.

We peered through the portholes in the swing doors. The sick people on the ward were all in bed, some reading, some listening to the radio on headphones, some watching the big TV set on a bracket high on the wall. At the entrance to the ward was the nurses' station, a nurse, her head bent, writing at the desk. In his bed, Taid was still flat on his back, his eyes closed.

'Right,' Twm said, getting the powder out of his pocket. I unslung the backpack and fished out my own packet. It was chilled from contact with the Egg. I hoped it wouldn't affect the way it worked!

'One, two, three – now!' Twm whispered, and we pushed through the swing doors like cowboys entering a saloon, only with fairy dust instead of Colt 45s.

We sprinted from bed to bed, sprinkling young blokes, old blokes, middle-aged blokes, willing them to forget they ever saw us. And because that's what the magic powder does – that is, exactly what you want it to – they all stared right through us with kind of goofy grins. The nurse looked up as we approached, and got up to tick us off for being on the ward way after visiting hours, but a face-full of fairy dust soon fixed her!

We reached Taid's bed and swished the drapes round. He opened his eyes at Twm's touch on his arm.

'About time, too,' he grumbled, sitting up. 'Where've you been, boy?'

'Couldn't just up and fetch you, Taid, could we?' he replied. 'Had to make some preparations, first.'

The old man shoved back the bedclothes and swung his pyjama'd legs over the bedside. 'Pass me my slippers. Under the locker, I expect,' he ordered, and I bent down to look. Good thing I did, because beneath the curtain I saw a pair of feet approaching. Large feet in high-heeled shiny black shoes. I peeked between the drapes.

Ms Mordreda Critchett. Now we were in trouble.

The drapes swished back. 'Well, well, well,' she began, her painted lips curving in an evil smile. 'What have we here? Three for the price of one!'

'Twm!' I gasped.

He whirled round, whisked the packet of powder out of his pocket and threw the remains of it over the woman.

It was quite disappointingly unspectacular, really. She twitched, her eyes crossed, and she slithered to the floor, where she lay like a rag doll, completely unconscious. That's the truly great thing about Taid's magic powder: it does just what you want it to do at the time that you throw it. Lucky for her Twm threw it and not me – she might have self-combusted if I'd done it!

'Quick,' Twm ordered. 'Before anyone else comes along, help me get Taid out of here!'

But when the old man tried to stand, he couldn't, his legs wouldn't hold him up.

'We need a wheelchair!' I said, and sprinted to find one. A folding one leaned against the wall in the treatment room, so I snapped it open and pelted along the corridor with it. Between us we lifted him into it, covered his legs with a blanket we snitched from a spare trolley, and headed for the exit. The only person we saw was a ward maid doing the cocoa rounds, and she was yawning so widely she didn't even see us. Within minutes we were down in the lift and outside in the parking lot. I pulled Mom's cellphone out of my backpack and called a cab. By the time I'd finished the call my fingers were numb with cold from the effects of the Egg on the phone.

The cab arrived and, leaving the wheelchair in the parking lot, we heaved Taid into the backseat. I sat beside him and Twm sat up front with the driver to give him directions. We paid him off at the cottage and between us managed to get Taid inside. He collapsed into his old armchair with a sigh of satisfaction.

'There, now,' he murmured, closing his eyes. 'Feel better already. Knew I would. Be as right as rain in the morning, you see if I'm not.' He was instantly asleep.

'I can't leave him,' Twm said. 'You take my bike and get on home. Oh, *Duw*, Catrin, I hope we've done the right thing!'

'Of course we have!' I said fiercely. 'How could we leave him in the hospital with a Spoiler about?'

'I know you're right, but –' he shrugged, helplessly.

'But nothing. Look at him! He's got more colour already! I'll be back in the morning.'

I pedalled off down the road on Twm's bike, the beam of the headlamp wavering on the road in front of me, illuminating flashes of green bush, and the startling neon eyes of a fox creeping along the verge.

I'd sort of forgotten the Spoilers' mansion was on the way home from Twm's place . . .

CHAPTER TWELVE

So there I was, pedalling along the dark lanes, my backpack chilly between my shoulderblades, whistling a kind of 'who's afraid of the big bad wolf?' whistle to keep my courage up. Then, I suddenly remembered I was about to pass Mrs Gwynne Davies' mansion in about two hundred metres time, and my level of courage, already well down thanks to getting dive-bombed by a hunting barn owl, whizzed down some more . . .

One time I'd been there at night on my own, the two big, ugly stone birds that sat one on each gatepost had come to life and chased me down the road. I was torn between getting off Twm's bike and tiptoeing past, and pedalling real fast to get past quicker! The bike was silent except for the faint *tic* that the turning wheels made, and I decided to opt for speed. I stood up on the pedals and shoved, hard. The gateposts, topped by the lumpy bird-shapes, loomed up on the left. I hardly dared look. But then, as I passed the tall black iron gates, couldn't resist a quick glance – like keeping one's eye on large spiders on the bedroom ceilings – and I saw a light on in the mansion . . .

I know, I know, I should have left well enough alone and gone right on back to the Toll House and safety. But I didn't, did I? And we *did* need to know what the Spoilers were plotting.

I concealed Twm's bike and my backpack (didn't want to risk taking the Egg close to the Spoilers) under a hedge, found a shadowy place on the wall and climbed over – no way was I gonna risk climbing the gates, or worse, opening them!

Carefully avoiding the gravel drive I tippy-toed over the lawn towards the lighted window, did a long-jump over the crunchy path onto the flower-bed outside, and stuck my ear against the pane. All I could hear was muffled voices – I couldn't make out what they were saying.

I had an idea of the layout of the mansion: after all, I'd been inside before, last time, to take the Egg back when the Spoilers had stolen it. I knew more or less which room was the sitting room, and which the kitchen, and decided to snoop round the back, see if I could hear anything. I crept round the side of the house. The lights were out at the back, and when I tried the handle of the kitchen door, it turned and opened a crack. I stuck my head inside and listened. Rats. The voices were still too muffled to make out words. I sighed. Nothing else for it then. Breaking-and-entering time again.

I shoved the door open and slipped silently inside. Something suddenly hummed loudly in the corner and I jumped about a foot in the air until I realised that it was only an icebox. I took a few steps closer to the door, able to see the outline of a table and kitchen units in the moonlight filtering through the lace curtains. I eased open the door into the hall and waited, not breathing, just listening.

'. . . girl back from France could have ruined everything,' I heard Mrs Gwynne Davies say. 'At least the old man is neutralised while he's in hospital. Mordreda will make sure he doesn't come out too soon – if he comes out at all!' She cackled horribly, and goosebumps travelled up my arms.

An unfamiliar man's voice spoke then. A young-sounding voice, maybe not much older than my own. 'If Mordreda takes care of the old man, I can take care of the girl. The most important thing is that now we know where the Sea King's Daughter is. Once we have her, we shall also have the three Signs and then we shall have it all. When we have driven them all away, then all of it – the power and the riches – will be ours.'

Three Signs? My heart lurched. *The Spoilers didn't know I still had the Sky Egg!* They must have thought I'd given all three back to the Sea Girl, and hadn't discovered that she'd given one to me.

'Tomorrow, my boy, we shall find the Sea Girl and then it will be almost over,' Mrs Gwynne Davies said, her voice thick with satisfaction. 'The American girl will be gone, soon, back to France, or better still, back to America. I shall see to that. A word from me in the right ear will ruin the whole family. Her father is here on a work permit, and I have friends in high places who are more than capable of arranging for him to be deported.' She cackled so hard that she began to cough, and under cover of the noise I turned and crept out again, just about incandescent with fury. Thought she could get my Dad deported, did she? Well, we'd see about that! We had friends in high places too, not least the American Ambassador in London! I was just easing the back door closed behind me when the sound of tyres on the gravel drive made me leap for the bushes to hide. Car headlights swept across the trees, but fortunately I was out of sight. I heard a car door slam, footsteps on the path, and the front door open and slam shut. And then, loud voices inside the house.

Nothing else for it. I crept back to the door and opened it again. This time I could hear perfectly well – they were yelling, was why!

'I tell you the old man has gone!' Mordreda Critchett was screaming. 'They took him from under my very nose! We have to get him back in the hospital. I can't understand why the stuff I put in his food didn't work! It should have made him so ill that an old man like him should have died! But he lived, and now he's escaped.'

'It's entirely your fault!' Mrs Gwynne Davies bawled back, 'if you'd done your part properly the old man would be dead! We have to find him. You've ruined all our plans. Well, it's your responsibility to find him and finish him off. He can't have gone far. Likely the boy has taken him home. Tomorrow we are going to find the Sea King's Daughter, get the Signs from her and finish this off. It can't wait any longer. And when you've seen to the old man, get rid of the boy. Get rid of all of them, every one, his brother, too. If I could find a way to reach her I'd finish off Nimue, as well. I've had more than enough of that brood interfering in my plans, and also more than enough of your incompetence, Critchett!'

Mordreda Critchett screamed furiously once, and slammed her way out of the living room. Time for a fast exit! I swiftly closed the door and ran like seven devils for the boundary wall. I scrambled over it, found Twm's bike and headed back along the road. I was gonna be real late getting home – but I had to warn Twm, get Taid out of the cottage before the morning, that was more important than Mom being mad at me.

It certainly couldn't wait until morning. I'd pedalled only a couple of hundred yards along the road when I was overtaken by Mrs Gwynne Davies' big, black car. Mordreda Critchett was at the wheel, driving so fast that she couldn't have seen me – not that she would have anyway, since by the time she drew level, I'd toppled off the bike, head first into a ditch at the sound of the engine behind me.

Covered in scratches and mud I picked myself up and gazed after the red tail-lights disappearing down the lane. I had no doubt where she was going: straight to Taid's, that's where. I had no chance of getting there first. I sat on the side of the road and groaned. We were beaten, and we'd hardly begun.

And then I felt the coldness of the Egg against my back, and remembered that, tucked in beside it, was the last little packet of Taid's fairy dust . . .

I scrabbled at the buckles, ripped open the bag, got out the little paper packet, wrestled it open, and sprinkled myself with the powder. Luckily I managed to grab the backpack with the Egg in it before the powder worked, because I was thinking, *speed of light, speed of light, speed of light.*

I never was a real good traveller. I felt quite motion-sick by the time I landed outside the cottage, but I knew I'd overtaken the car. Travelling at fast-forward speed makes me dizzy! I battered at the cottage door and hollered. An electric light went on in the house opposite and curtains twitched up and down the village, but at last a window opened upstairs and Twm's head appeared.

'Catrin? What are you doing here at this time of night?'

'Let me in, quick. We've got to get Taid outa here, or at least hide him someplace! Mordreda Critchett's on her way. She's after you – and Cei, too!'

Twm's head disappeared, feet pounded on stairs, and the door was flung open. 'Quick, come in!' he whispered, grabbing my arm and hauling me inside. 'Get a couple of packets of Taid's powder and come upstairs. I'll wake Taid.'

I hustled into the little living room and flung open the cupboard. There wasn't a whole lot left, but I snatched up what there was and headed upstairs with it. I could hear the sound of a car approaching . . .

Taid, in snazzy striped p.j's, was sitting up in bed rubbing his eyes. Twm was gabbling in his ear, and Taid was ignoring him. I heard the car stop outside.

'Quick!' I moaned, 'she's here!'

'Who's here? The Critchett woman? Does she think she can beat me? In my own home?'

120

'Yes, Taid, she probably can right now,' Twm said urgently. 'You're ill, remember? Your powers are weaker than they should be. Get out of bed and shut up, Taid, please.'

The three of us fell silent while Twm opened the packets of dust and sprinkled them over us. Taid and Twm disappeared, and although I could see myself, I knew I had, too. Weird stuff, that powder. I could see my own self, but no one else could. I heard Taid get out of bed and the slow shuffle of his bare feet across the floor. The bedroom door opened and closed, and I was alone in the room.

Then there was silence. I tried to slow my own breathing, because I was out of breath from panic and hurry, fear making my heart pound. The coldness of the Egg seeped through the backpack and I shivered.

The front door creaked open, and almost silently, feet came up the stairs. But if feet don't belong to a house, they don't know which floorboards, which stairs, creak, and so Mordreda's progress up the stairs was given away. Then the bedroom door slowly opened, and there she was in the doorway, her eyes glittering, her long red talons glinting in the electric light.

'Where is he?' she hissed, and stepped into the room. 'Where's he gone?' She looked carefully around. She sniffed, like an animal scenting its prey. 'I know you're here, old man. Come out. I won't hurt you. But you should be back in hospital, you know. You're sick!'

She crossed to the bed and ran her hand over the

bottom sheet. 'Warm! I knew it! Where are you, Merlin, you old fool? Don't you know when you're beaten?'

I held my breath as she prowled the room, feeling around for Taid as if she were playing blind man's buff.

'Where is he?' she muttered. 'How did he know I was coming? Unless –' She stopped, suddenly. 'Perhaps the boy has taken him somewhere else. Perhaps he realised that I would come looking for him here. Yes, that must be it! But they can only just have gone, the bed is warm. Now, where would he take him so late at night?'

She sat on the edge of the bed and tapped one red nail against a front tooth. 'Not back to hospital, that's certain. So where? Perhaps the girl's house. The Toll House. If he's there, we'll have him tomorrow, that's no problem. Yes, that's it. The Toll House. The American woman will have taken him in. We'll see to him there.'

Smiling, satisfied that she'd worked out the problem, she stood up and stretched. 'I shall have you soon, old man,' she said into the empty air. 'Wherever you hide, I shall find you. There are only three of you, and there are always four of Us. You will not beat us this time.' She clattered down the stairs and the front door slammed behind her. The car engine started, and I crossed to the window to watch the big motor purr down the road away from the cottage.

The bedroom door opened and shut, and gradually, from the toes up, Taid and Twm reappeared. The old man's face was grumpy.

'Thinks she's beaten us, does she? Well, that's what she thinks. Got a few tricks up my sleeve yet, I have.'

'I know, Taid. But what did she mean, she'll have you at the Toll House? How can she?'

I shrugged. 'Don't know. But I do know that Mrs Gwynne Davies is going to find the Sea Girl tomorrow. She knows where she is, Twm! So if we follow her, we'll find her too!'

'If we follow the Spoiler, we'll be too late. We have to get to her first. We have to persuade her to give us the Signs before it's too late. Oh, I wish I knew what we were up against!'

'Well, at least we know the third Spoiler is a guy. From his voice he's quite young.'

'That's a start. We can keep our eyes open for him. But I wonder who the fourth one is?'

CHAPTER THIRTEEN

'But where can Taid go for safety?' I asked. 'He could have come to the Toll House, I know Mom wouldn't think twice about asking him, but that's the first place they're gonna look, they said so. And no way can he go back in that hospital!'

Taid was pottering about his bedroom, packing stuff into an ancient black bag. He was looking way better than he had in the hospital bed, no doubt about that, but he still had that kind of frail look, and that worried me.

Twm scratched his head. 'Oh, *Duw,* I don't know. The problems seem to be multiplying by the minute. We don't know where the Sea Girl is, and there's Taid, and we still don't know what the Spoilers are after – or even who all of them are.'

Taid snapped the bag shut and buckled the strap. 'Would either of you care to consult me?' he asked mildly, 'because I'm not dead or entirely decrepit just yet, and I just might have an opinion, mightn't I? Catrin, *cariad* put the kettle on the hob, I need a cup of tea after all the excitement. Blackcurrant and camomile, please, to calm my nerves. In the blue jar there. Twm, fetch me this morning's *Western Mail, bachgen.* I think I can tell you what the Spoilers are after.' Taid sank into his high-backed armchair with a sigh.

I made a pot of tea which smelled gorgeous, but when I poured myself a cup, tasted foul. I'd rather have screaming nerves than drink that stuff! I noticed he heaped in the brown sugar, though, and added something from a bottle!

Twm came back with the newspaper. Taid perched his little half-moon glasses on the end of his nose and leafed through it, grunted with satisfaction, folded the paper in half and then in half again, and handed it to Twm, tapping an article with his finger. 'There,' he said, 'that's what they're after.'

I peered over Twm's shoulder.

OIL EXPLORATION IN CARDIGAN BAY
PERMISSION REFUSED

Oil corporation Topflite were yesterday refused permission to search for reserves of underwater oil in Cardigan Bay. Lawyers, backed by the environmental protection organisations Greenpeace and local group S.O.S.S. (Save Our Sea Shores) successfully blocked the company's proposals to use seismic testing to identify the location of oil within the Bay because of the likely effects on the area's wildlife. Topflite refused to comment after the hearing, but a press notice issued later stated that an appeal against the decision would be made.

'What's seismic testing?' I asked. 'I thought seismic was something to do with earthquakes, yeah?'

'Well, yes,' Twm said, putting the paper down. 'Same sort of principle, I suppose. What they do is, they tow big guns behind ships and fire compressed air into the water as they go. They pick up the echoes from the seabed, and that way their geologists can work out where there's oil.'

I still didn't see the problem. 'But if they aren't shooting the guns *at* anything, and it's only air anyhow, then what's the problem? I mean, I guess there's oil there, but it's a long way from finding the stuff to getting it off the seabed, right? And if they aren't shooting at anything, how can it harm the wildlife?'

'Oh, it can,' Twm said. 'All the wildlife from fish to birds will be aware of it at the very least, but worst of all, the dolphins will suffer terribly. Their whole existence is built around sound signals, Catrin. They speak to each other over long distances, keep in touch with their group and navigate and find food with sound. If their sonar is disturbed, all that will go haywire. They'll be so disoriented, they'll either leave the Bay – or starve to death. And the same goes for the seals. Loud noises will drive them away from the area and away from the places where they come ashore to birth their pups.'

'Oh, shoot!' I breathed. 'Taid, do you think the Spoilers are behind this?'

Taid nodded. 'More than likely they are behind this company, Topflite. There's lots of money in oil, Catrin, and there's nothing the Spoilers like better than money.'

'So now we know why the dolphin was lured ashore the other night,' Twm said. 'If the Spoilers can make the dolphins unhappy, make them uncomfortable, put them in danger, perhaps they think they'll leave of their own accord, and then their appeal to be allowed to carry out this seismic testing will get the go-ahead. No dolphins, no problem.'

'They're trying to drive the dolphins away?' I said, outraged. 'Twm, we've got to stop them! Tell someone!'

'Who'd listen?' he said, simply. 'We have to find the Sea Girl's Signs, first, and then get proof of what they're doing. Then we can tell someone. Without the Signs, you know as well as I do, no one will believe us.'

'Right, OK,' I said, anger and determination firing me up. 'Let's get going, find the Sea Girl, get the Signs. But first – what about Taid?'

'Me?' The old man stroked his beard smooth, and put a woolly bobble hat on top of his wild hair. 'I'm going home, that's where I'm going.'

'Home?' I said, stupidly. 'Isn't this home?'

And then I remembered the cave, high in the mountains of Snowdonia, where tapestries hung on walls, lighted torches illuminated glistening walls, and a great Mirror lay, veiled with red cloth. I grinned. 'Oh, yeah! Home.' I picked up Taid's bag. 'You'll be OK there, Taid.'

'And if we consult my Mirror,' Taid suggested, 'you might – how do you say it in America, Catrin? – get a drop on the bad guys.'

Twm locked the cottage door behind us, and we stood in the darkness. I looked at my watch: nearly two a.m. Mom was gonna throw a hissy fit over this.

If she didn't kill me straight off. The Mommy-nose was gonna be white as snow.

Taid saw me glance at my watch. 'Don't worry, Catrin, your Mam is fast asleep. She won't even know you're gone, I promise.'

I was about to say, 'and how can you promise that?' when I saw the twinkle in his eye. Of course he could! He could promise just about anything he wanted – he was Merlin, wasn't he?'

The three of us, me with my backpack and the Egg, Taid with his old-fashioned bag, and Twm, stood together in the little flowery front garden. Taid handed Twm the last two packets of powder.

'You do the honours, boy,' he said, 'taller than the rest of us, you can make it go further.'

Twm sprinkled, and I made a picture in my head of the cave, and in a split second I was airborne, rushing through space like a UFO, my hair streaming back, my eyes watering at the speed of it, with Twm and Taid on each side of me. And then we were there, outside the cave, the giant oak tree in full leaf.

Twm reached up for the key hidden on its ledge and unlocked the door. The cave was just as I remembered it: rushes under our feet, crystals glittering in the rock walls in the light of dozens of burning torches, the roof arching high above us. There was the intricately carved high-backed chair, the simple bed covered in sheepskins, and the cloak on a peg on the wall . . .

On a vast table occupying the centre of the cavern, was a mirror, covered in red cloth.

Taid threw his bag on the wooden bed, took off his hat, untucked his beard from inside his coat and fluffed it out, adjusted his spectacles and looked both several centuries younger and very businesslike, both at once. He also looked a whole lot healthier!

'*Nawr te!*' he said, 'Twm?'

They each took two corners of the cloth and lifted it off the mirror. Twm folded the cloth neatly and stacked it away on the chair beside the bed. The mirror gleamed in the torchlight, reflecting the jewel-coloured wall hangings.

The three of us bent over the glass and peered in.

'What exactly are we looking for?' I whispered.

Twm spoke in a normal voice. 'You don't have to whisper, you aren't in church and nobody but us is listening. We're looking for the Sea King's Daughter, of course. If we can find her, maybe we can get to her before the Spoilers do.'

Taid/Merlin gave the mirror a rub with his sleeve. 'Come on, Catrin. You look. You're the Sea Girl too, after all.'

I knew that. I really did. But somehow it still seemed so unreal that I could be two people in one skin – Catrin Rhys Morgan, and somehow the Sea Girl, too.

I searched the shining surface for a trace of my other Self. Mists swirled within the mirror, and suddenly there was a rapid succession of images – a stormy sea, a bleak, windswept shore, a wood in winter, stark black branches tracing a sky leaden with snow. Nothing I recognised, nothing that gave us a clue where the Sea King's Daughter was.

'Where can she *be*?' I groaned, and rubbed my eyes. More images: a body of water and offshore, a long, low island. A small cottage at the edge of the sea, so close to the tide-line that seaweed had blown against the whitewashed walls.

'That's where she is,' Taid said, matter-of-factly.

'But where?' Twm asked.

'The mirror is showing us her journey,' Taid said. 'First the sea, then the shore, then a wood, now a cottage.'

'Great,' I muttered, 'but which bit of seashore, which wood, and how do we find the cottage?'

'Easy,' Taid said, straightening his back. 'You've seen the cottage – all you have to do is visualise it and you're there. Just like coming here.'

'But we don't have any of the powder left, do we? I asked.

'Powder? Don't need powder when I'm in my cave, girl! Got more magic in this cave than you have dreamed of in your philosophy, Horatio!' the old man chuckled. 'Tidy turn of phrase, that young Shakespeare fellow!'

I thought for a minute the old guy had flipped, but then realised he was so old he might have gotten schlocked in a tavern some time in the past with old Will himself!

Taid opened a large wooden cupboard in the corner of the cave and started rummaging about in its depths. He brought out a small leather bag, untied the strings and beckoned us over.

'Hands,' he ordered, and obediently we stretched

them out. Into each of our palms fell a small object that rattled. It looked at first like a miniature bracelet made from tiny, white sections of bamboo – but then I realised they were actually dried fish backbones!

'Fishbones?' I said, confused. 'What good are fishbones?'

'Not just *any* fishbones,' Taid explained. 'Fishbones from the salmon of all the rivers of Wales. Salmon have magical properties – they are the king of fish, and the rivers of Wales once teemed with them. There is a bone here from the first salmon that ever swam in each one of the rivers: the Wye, the Clwyd, the Usk, the Cothi, the Dee, dozens more, every single one that ever held a salmon. Each bone will work once. Place one on your tongue and concentrate. Don't swallow it or throw it away after – it can be recharged to use again.'

I opened my mouth but he held up his hand to shut me up.

'No time for questions, Catrin. Find the Sea Girl.'

I just hoped that when we found her, she'd cooperate . . .

CHAPTER FOURTEEN

I left the Sky Egg with Taid. If anything went wrong when we found the Sea Girl, it would be safer with him than risking it falling into the Spoilers' hands. I slipped a section of fish backbone off the bracelet and looked at it. Didn't much fancy putting it in my mouth, but Twm didn't seem to have any such problem: well, what did I have to lose? I opened up and popped a fishbone.

What did I have to lose? My supper, that's what! I instantly felt real sick and dizzy, and reached out for Twm for support. He was reaching for me at the same time, so we kind of held on to each other until the dizzy feeling passed.

'What was *that*?' I muttered uneasily.

'Magic,' he said shortly, grabbing my hand. 'Now hang on. Just get a picture of the cottage in your mind and hang on to it. Close your eyes and concentrate hard.'

Obediently I closed my eyes and pictured the cottage as I'd seen it in the mirror.

Then I felt sick again, there was a loud rushing sound, a feeling of falling over, and when I opened my eyes we were standing (or rather, tottering) outside a tiny, whitewashed cottage. I spat the fishbone into my hand and slipped it back onto the bracelet. There would be no difficulty picking it out from the unused ones: it had turned black as ebony. It left a musty, fishy taste in my mouth. Yuk.

I looked about me. The cottage was slate-roofed, one-storey, with a window each side of the door like in a child's drawing. It had been built with half of it below ground level, looking as if it had been too heavy for the foundations, and had sunk into the ground like a heavy birthday candle into soft cake-frosting. A grassy bank rose up all around it like a wall to protect it from the sea-winds. Only the shiny grey roof projected, like some scaly beast crouching in the coarse sea-grass.

Inside the cottage, someone was singing. There were no words to the song, it was just the rise and fall of sound. There didn't seem to be a melody to it, but all the same it was familiar. Oh, what was it? I knew it so well . . .

Whales! She was singing whalesong! The weird, sweet, pinging, moaning song of a humpback, unless I was mistaken. Twm looked down at me and grinned.

'Whalesong?' I whispered.

'Of course!' he said. 'She knows them all.'

We opened the gate set at the bottom of the sloping groove down to the front door. The house was surrounded by only a bare metre of land before the hillside rose again to encircle it, but of course no flowers would grow where sun couldn't reach. Instead, there were thousands and thousands of perfect shells of all description: twisted cornet shells, oysters, cockles, milky blue mussels, jewelled, chequered sea-snails, arranged in intricate patterns to form a mosaic of colour and texture. I knew instinctively that the Sea-Girl had done it: perhaps an attempt to fight off homesickness for her undersea kingdom. On the grassy bank at the right hand side of the house, draped over a wooden frame, hung a fishing net dotted with cork floats, and a pile of lobster pots stood neatly alongside.

Twm knocked on the door, and the singing stopped. There was silence from inside the cottage: the sort of silence and stillness you get when someone is listening hard, and is real afraid of something. The sort of silence and stillness you get when a wild creature is trying to pretend it isn't there at all so a predator will go away without eating it.

When no one answered his knock, Twm put his hand on the latch and gently lifted it. The door swung wide into a tiny, spotless, empty room. We stepped inside and looked around us. A table, two chairs, a rag rug similar to the one on the floor of the Toll House, stone flags, a black-leaded hob with a kettle propped on it, and a blackened pot on a hook over the fire. And in the farthest wall, a closed door.

We listened. Something rustled behind the door. 'Sea Girl?' I called, 'Are you there? We don't mean to scare you, but we really need to talk with you.'

There was silence again, so Twm tried. 'It's me, Twm ap Myrddin. Don't be afraid, we won't harm you. We must talk to you. We need the Signs.'

There was movement behind the door, and slowly it opened a crack. One huge green eye peered round, and then the door opened fully, and the Sea Girl was there, staring at us.

She looked kinda wrong on land. She was so thin –
her wrists were the size of a child's – and her dark
hair clung lankly to her face instead of floating free to
frame it as it did underwater. She was greenish pale,
and she walked awkwardly, as if her feet hurt her.
She'd been so beautiful, so natural in her own habitat
beneath the tide, but here, in this poor little cottage,
she was out of place as she could be. She looked
weak and sickly and very, very unhappy.

'What do you want?' Her voice was soft and
breathy, like seafroth-bubbles bursting on sand.

'Do you remember Catrin?' Twm asked softly.
'You gave her the Sky Egg.'

The Sea Girl glanced at me and a small smile
flickered. 'Yes.' Pale eyelids fluttered over the green
eyes. 'You are the other Me.'

'That's right!' I said, delighted that she recalled our
meeting.

'What do you want, Twm ap Myrddin?' she asked.

'We need the Sea Harp and the Earthstone,' Twm
said. 'The Spoilers are back, and they will destroy
your father's kingdom if they are allowed to.'

'Nothing can destroy the Kingdom of the Sea,' she
said dismissively. 'My father rules everything beneath
the waves. Even the moon pays homage to him.'

Actually, I'd thought it was kind of the other way
about, the moon ruling the tides, but what did I know?

'The Spoilers may not destroy it entirely, but they
mean to drive away all that inhabits it, seals, dolphins,
shark. The great rafts of Manx shearwaters will not
return, the puffins and cormorants and tern will all

disappear, if the Spoilers have their way. And in their place there will be great ships filled with thick, black oil. If the Sea King shows his anger and breaks them up, his kingdom will be poisoned, ruined, gone forever.'

The Sea Girl put her head on one side. 'My father will do as he wishes. I am no longer his child. I cannot go home. He has forgotten me. I chose to have legs. I chose to walk in dust. This is my world now.'

'Why?' I asked. 'Why can't you go home? I'm sure your father would forgive you. He loves you. All Dads love their kids, no matter what they do.'

'But I am married to a human,' she whispered, the great, green eyes flooding. 'Dewi, his name is. I promised him that I would not seek the flowing tides, or swim with the seals or fly with the dolphins. In return he made me his wife.'

'But you can't just turn your back on the sea!' I said, horrified. 'You're the Sea King's Daughter! The Sea Girl! You have responsibilities!'

She shook her head. 'I have no responsibilities. You are also the Sea Girl. You guard it. I am exiled from the Sea.'

Twm butted in, then. 'Are you happy, Sea Girl, away from your father and the creatures of the sea?'

She stared at him. 'What is happy? I am here. I have legs. My husband must love me, for he visits me sometimes and brings me food, and shells for my sea-garden. I ask nothing more. He is away now, but I shall see him soon, I expect. Perhaps this is happiness.'

'Sea Girl, there is very little time,' Twm argued, 'the Spoilers are coming to find you. Please, give us the Signs. We have the Sky Egg, but we need the others, too. If you don't give them to us, the Spoilers will take them, and the dolphins will be driven from the Bay forever. Do you want that?'

She covered her mouth with her hands, the enormous green eyes gazing at him. 'The Spoilers are coming here?' she whimpered. 'I must hide! Oh, help me, please help me! I shall die if the Spoilers find me!'

I suddenly had an idea. It might work, but it was a long shot. 'Sea Girl, let us hide you. We can take you somewhere safe. But you must give us the Signs.'

'If I give them to you, and let you hide me,' she said slowly, 'will you promise to care for them?'

'Of course I will,' I said, trying to look honest and trustworthy. 'Of course. After all, I'm just as much the Sea Girl as you are.'

'But you have legs,' she said softly, 'and I do not. My legs are just an illusion. If I stop concentrating for one minute on the magic that makes them, they will vanish, and I shall be a fish-woman again. Then my husband will leave me. He could not love a fish-woman.'

Suddenly, I heard the unmistakable sound of a car engine. I looked out of the window: Mrs Gwynne Davies's monster auto was jolting over the rough sea-turf towards the cottage.

'They're coming!' I hissed, grabbing Twm's arm. 'We've got to get the Signs and get out of here.'

The Sea Girl went even paler than before. 'Oh, what shall I do?' she moaned.

'Give us the Signs, quickly,' I ordered. 'We can't stay – the Spoilers are coming, right now!' I'd just about had enough of her dithering. We needed to get out of there, fast!

She whirled, her brown dress flying up, revealing her thin legs. The illusion that held them was not a strong one: their outline wavered and blurred. She ran into the back room and came back clutching a leather bag and a small iron box: the Sea Harp and the Earthstone.

'Gotcha!' I muttered under my breath. Now let's get out of here!

Twm grabbed the bag and the box and shoved them inside his jacket, zipping it up over the top of them. 'Quick, Catrin, give the Sea Girl one of your bones. Let's get her back to Taid.'

I slipped two off, handed one to her and put the other in my mouth. Twm grabbed her left hand, I grabbed her right, and we both concentrated hard on Taid. As the sick feeling hit, the Sea Girl moaned, and tried to pull free, but luckily she didn't think to spit out the bone, and Twm and I held on tight.

Lurch, stumble, yuk, and when I opened my eyes we were, all three of us, plus the Signs, back in the cave. Taid was waiting for us in his rocking chair, sipping a cup of tea and eating a sandwich. When we appeared he put down his cup and opened his arms. The Sea Girl rushed into them.

'Ah, *cariad*, he crooned. 'There's a long way from

home you are. You will be safe with me, *Ferch-y-Môr*. And who knows, eh? Maybe I can persuade you to go back to your Dada, mmm?'

'My father will not have me back,' she sighed. 'He does not want a daughter with legs.'

'And your husband does not want a wife with a tail, is that it?' Taid chuckled. 'Well, *ferch*, there's a pickle!'

'Taid,' Twm broke in urgently. 'We've got the Signs, all three of them, now. What do we do next?'

'Well, boy, you use them, don't you?'

CHAPTER FIFTEEN

'Use them how?' I said, blankly.

'We don't know that, do we?' Twm said patiently. 'We have to wait and see what the Spoilers do next, and then we can try to stop them doing it. Whatever it is.'

'So we have to wait until they hurt a dolphin or something, or drive another one onto the beach? Next time maybe we won't be so lucky and won't get to it in time!' I said indignantly. 'Like, I don't think so, Twm! We so need to be out there fighting them. We can't just sit around waiting like bumps on a log!'

Twm sighed. 'That's what I think, too, Catrin, but where do we start? We have to be ready for whatever they do, but we haven't got anything to go on, have we? After all, we don't know who the other two Spoilers are, we haven't got any proof of what they are going to do – we only *think* it's to do with oil. Until we can prove to ourselves what they're up to, how can we hope to prove it to anyone else?'

'We've got the Signs, now!' I protested, 'can't we just go *zap* 'em?'

'No, we can't. Suppose we botch it, and underwater oil in Cardigan Bay isn't what they're after?' Twm explained patiently. 'What do we do then? We've shown our hand, and used the Signs. It makes us vulnerable. What if we're wrong about the oil? What if it's something else entirely?'

'You really think it could be?' I asked doubtfully.

'No, not really. I'm pretty sure Taid's right and it's oil they're after. It's worth millions if it's there. But at the moment they don't know we've got the Signs, and they don't know we've got the Sea Girl.'

'She does have a name,' Taid put in, mildly. 'You might like to use it occasionally, instead of just calling her Sea Girl.'

'If I knew it, I'd use it,' I said, scowling.

Taid said something quite unintelligible.

'Pardon me?' I said. 'Run that past me again, please.'

He did. I still didn't get it. It had a sort of whispery, wet, splashy sound to it, and I didn't think my vocal chords would ever manage it.

Taid chuckled. 'Call her Mallt,' he suggested. 'That's the closest you'll get, I think.'

'Mallt,' I said. 'Is that OK, Sea Girl?'

She nodded, pink with pleasure.

'Is that what your husband calls you?' I asked.

The big green eyes filled up again, and she shook her head. 'He calls me just Girl,' she whispered. 'Girl. As if I had no name at all.'

I exchanged a glance with Twm. He looked blank. 'Erm. Could I have a word outside, Twm?' I suggested.

Outside the cave, I picked up a pebble and chucked it down the mountain, clattering and bouncing. 'Kinda unfriendly, husband-to-wife, wouldn't you say? Girl?'

'Well, I suppose, so. But I don't see the problem.'

Guys! 'Twm, folks that are in love, they have little

141

pet names for each other. They don't just call each other 'girl' and 'boy'. They call each other snookie-ookums, and cutie pumpkin, and sugar-pie, stuff like that.'

'They do?' Twm looked vaguely nauseous.

'Trust me on that one, Twm. Sure they do. So doesn't it seem kinda weird that the Sea G-, sorry, Mallt's husband just calls her Girl, like she's a dog or something?'

'I suppose. But I don't get your point.'

'Think about this. Suppose Mallt's husband doesn't really love her? Suppose he wants something from her. Suppose he hasn't really married her – after all, what does a Sea King's daughter know about human customs? Suppose, just suppose, he was after the Signs.'

Twm stared at me. 'You mean Mallt's husband might be a –'

'Spoiler. Exactly, Twm.'

'So why didn't he just take the signs from her?'

'He didn't need to, did he? They were right there, ready for him when he needed them. He had the Sea Girl, what more did he need? Only maybe he didn't know she only had two of them.'

'Bit far-fetched, Catrin, if you ask me.'

'OK, yeah, but you see my point, don't you?'

'Well yes, but – well, with respect, Catrin, so what?'

'So what? Well, if I'm right, then we've at least identified another Spoiler, which means we have three of them now. It also means that if we can prove to Mallt that this guy doesn't really love her, maybe we can get her to go back to her father.'

142

'So, how do we prove it?'

I grinned smugly. 'Eavesdrop. We creep up on them and we listen. That way we can find out exactly what their plans are, and who the other Spoilers are for sure, and once we know what they're planning to do, we can make sure they don't do it.'

He scratched his head. 'I suppose it's an idea.'

'Got a better one?'

He shook his head.

'Come on then.'

'Where?'

'Back to Mallt's cottage. Only this time, we take some of Taid's fairy dust so the Spoilers can't see us!'

Taid had plenty of the magical brownish powder, so Twm and I both put a half-dozen little packets in various pockets about our persons, just in case. Then we got out the fish-bones again. Oh, putting those in my mouth was, like, so *gross.*

All the same, gross or not, it worked. Nauseating nanoseconds later, we were outside the cottage again, and Twm sprinkled the two of us with dust, both of us thinking, *invisible, invisible,* until we were. The big, flashy auto was parked outside, the doors were open, and loud voices were shouting.

'Why is it,' Mrs Gwynne Davies's harsh croak asked, 'that you are all so utterly incompetent? You are incapable of doing the simplest things! I told you, Dewi, to stay with the girl, make sure that she and the Signs stayed put, but you left her alone, and now she has gone. Goodness knows where she is.'

An unfamiliar voice shouted back. 'I told her not to

go gallivanting off, but she's thick as two short planks. She was wanting to go to market the other day. I soon put that out of her head, I can tell you! But you can't expect me to stay round here all day just to watch her wimping around the place.'

'She's your wife, you imbecile! This is where you should be! Have you no sense at all?' Mrs Gwynne Davies shrieked in reply.

'She's not my wife. Only thinks she is. What, d'you think I'd marry something that's half-fish? Gives me the willies just to think about it.'

Miss Critchett's voice, silkily sinister, joined in. 'You were well paid to watch her. Well, where do you suggest we look for her? She isn't here, is she?'

'We don't need the Girl. It's the Signs we want!' Mrs Gwynne Davies hissed. 'The Girl can go hang for all I care. Where are the damned Signs?'

We drifted invisibly in through the cottage door and watched the Spoilers ransack the cottage. The Sea Girl's 'husband' was about twenty-five, dark-haired, handsome in a petulant way. He stood, hands in jeans pockets, watching the other two search.

'Where did she hide them, Dewi?' Miss Critchett asked him, thrusting her face close up to his so that he backed away. I guess it's called 'invading his personal space', and he didn't like it a whole lot. Besides, Miss Critchett sprayed when she talked . . .

'How should I know?'

'Didn't you live here? Didn't you watch her?'

'What, me live here? You've got to be joking, Critchett.' Dewi shuddered in disgust.

144

Mrs Gwynne Davies turned on him. 'You were paid to watch her, Dewi. You were told not to let her out of the house. Where were you?'

Dewi scratched his head. 'Down the pub. Like I said, it was boring round here, no telly or anything. What was I supposed to do for laughs? And she kept singing those weird songs of hers. Gave me the creeps, it did. Anyway, I told her to stay put, and mostly she did. Her legs weren't much good for walking on, so I knew she couldn't get far. I brought her fish and stuff, and shells – she likes shells, they helped keep her quiet – and she did as she was told.' He sniggered unpleasantly. 'Told her I was going off to sea. She didn't know any better. So she stayed here and I checked up on her every couple of days.'

'But she brought the Signs with her, didn't she?'

He shrugged. 'Suppose so. How was I supposed to know? She put her stuff in the bedroom. Like a little kid, she was, opening and shutting drawers and putting stuff away. If I'd gone and asked her if she had the Signs, when she first moved in, she might have got suspicious, mightn't she?'

'But if you had, or if you'd just found them and taken them, we'd have the Signs by now, and the Sea Girl wouldn't matter. You are absolutely useless, Dewi. I knew we shouldn't have trusted a half-wit like you.'

'Half-wit? Thanks a lot. Let me remind you that all you told me to do was make her fall in love with me, that's all. Well, I did that. She stayed here, did what she was told. You never said anything about finding

145

the Signs. I thought you knew where they were. It's not my fault if she's done a runner.'

'How could she run, you imbecile? She doesn't have any legs! As soon as she stops concentrating, she's 50% fish again! She can't run anywhere, can she?' Mrs Gwynne Davies's temper was reaching spontaneous combustion point. She was purple in the face and the hairy wart on her face was wiggling like a live bug.

'If she can't run anywhere,' Dewi pointed out, 'then where is she? Either she's gone back to the sea, or she's invisible.'

'Or someone's taken her,' Miss Critchett suggested suddenly. 'Someone, perhaps, who is also interested in the Signs.'

Mrs Gwynne Davies stopped hyperventilating and calmed down. 'You mean the boy?'

'Or his grandfather. And the girl is back from France, of course. The two of them managed to spirit the old man out of the hospital. Maybe they've done the same for the Sea Girl. Maybe they've got her.'

'Where would they take her?' Dewi asked.

'If they've got her, mark my words, she'll be nowhere we can lay hands on her. And if they've got her, they will have the Signs, as well. But they can't stay hidden forever. The American girl will have to go home to the Toll House some time, and we already have a Spoiler inside there. As soon as she returns to her dreadful family, why then, we'll have her. And once we have her, we shall soon have the Sea Girl, the Signs – and the old man and the boy at our mercy.'

Mrs Gwynne Davies cackled. 'So, all is not lost, not just yet. Come along. We have plenty to do. I think we should take our tape machine and pay a visit to the seashore tonight. I am sure there will be a family of dolphin and a porpoise or two just waiting to be entertained. And this time there will be no interference from the boy and his friends.'

CHAPTER SIXTEEN

Miss Critchett, Mrs Gwynne-Davies and Dewi left, slamming the cottage door behind them. When the big black car had driven off, Twm and I reappeared. Twm was pale.

'Looks like you're right about the oil, Twm,' I said, 'they're gonna go pick on the dolphins again. What can we do? We have to warn them!'

Twm chewed the inside of his lip. 'That's no problem. I can find them easily and tell them what's going on. Tell them not to answer or follow if anyone calls their Sea-Names. No, it's the other thing they said that's really worrying me.'

'What?'

'Weren't you listening? They were talking about you.'

'Well, yeah, but I was so busy worrying about the Sea-Girl and the dolphins and stuff I guess I missed some of it. So, what?'

'They said it didn't matter about you. That they have somebody *inside* the Toll House to keep an eye on you.'

I stared at him. 'They said that?'

'Yes, they did. So, who?'

'Oh, Twm, you can't think it's Walt! No way is it him!'

'But there is only Walt. But I was so sure he was

one of us. I felt it when we shook hands, and when we got that dolphin back out to sea, he was with us every step of the way, and the dolphin was fine with him. But unless it's your Dad or your Mam or Jake, I suppose it has to be Walt.'

'I wouldn't put *much* past Jake, but I can quite positively state that none of my family would do anything so awful as be a Spoiler.' I felt quite insulted that he had even thought of it. 'Are you sure that's what they said?'

'Positive. Look, Catrin, perhaps the best thing would be to split up. I'll go back and tell Taid what's happening, then I'll take my boat and go and find the dolphins. You go home and start being suspicious.'

'Suspicious, how?'

'Well, you could search Walt's room. He's staying with you, isn't he? Maybe there's some kind of evidence. Documents or something, I don't know.'

'Yeah. But Twm, I just know it isn't him!'

'I hope it isn't, because if it is, it means my instincts are all messed up. But who else is there?'

We each popped another bit of fishbone, but headed in different directions this time. I found myself outside the Toll House under the bent old tree in the garden in back of the house. I could see Mom in the kitchen, but no way did I want her to know I was back. I sneaked round to the side of the house, where the old stone staircase is. The Toll House is so old that once upon a time there weren't inside stairs – the people that lived there had to go outside to go up to bed, which must have been a real pain in the rain!

Because the house was a Listed Building, the outside stairway had to stay, and the door at the top led to Jake's room. It was always kept locked, and Dad kept the key on his key ring, not because he thought Jake might sneak out one dark night and go adventuring, but because he KNEW he would, given half a chance! However, I still had some of Taid's dust, so a little locked door was no problem, right?

I was inside Jake's hell-hole in seconds. My room is no monument to me as a tidy person, but Jake's was a *tip*. I tiptoed across the floor, avoiding the creaky board that ran from Jake's room, under the wall and into mine, opened the door and peered across the landing. I knew Dad and Walt were out, and it looked like Mom was the only one at home. I could hear her warbling along to an old Beach Boys song on the radio.

I crept across to Walt's room. The door was closed, and I opened it quickly, remembering how it creaked if it was opened slowly. A quick, short noise would be less likely to be heard than a long, drawn-out one, especially over ancient pop-song music.

Walt's room was the complete opposite of Jake's, being pin-neat and with everything put away. The only thing of his that was out on view was a large dream-catcher hanging on his bed-post, almost identical to the one he wore round his neck. I took a deep breath, still not believing that the big man could be a bad guy, and turned myself into Catrin the Spy.

I felt awful, snooping in his closet and highboy drawers. I swiftly opened and shut, opened and shut, taking only moments to sift through piles of undershorts, socks, shirts, t-shirts and all the other stuff guys keep in their closets. There was nothing suspicious there at all. Downstairs Tom Jones was bellowing away now, and I sat on the bed and looked round me. There was nothing on top of the closet, nothing under the bed (not even dust – Mom the home-maker strikes again!). I had an idea, and started removing drawers, peering at the underside of each in case something had been taped there, the way they do in movies to hide Last Wills and Testaments, stuff like that. I was so engrossed in this I wasn't paying attention. I vaguely noticed that old Tom had been switched off in the middle of the 'Green, Green Grass of Home', but my heart almost stopped when the bedroom door opened and Walt appeared.

He looked mildly surprised to see me sitting on his bed. He halted in the doorway and blinked. Then he came in, stood on the rug with his hands shoved in his Levis pockets and said, 'Hi, Catrin! Can I help you with something?'

I felt my face burning up, and I opened and shut my mouth like a goldfish. I was like, so, so, majorly embarrassed! I couldn't think of anything at all to say to justify my presence in his private space. Then I heard voices downstairs: Dad and Mom, and a third voice I didn't recognise. Leaping off the duvet, I mumbled, 'Oh, wow! Visitors! Must go, Walt! Good to see you!' or some such nonsense, shot past him and down the stairs.

I halted at the bottom to get my equilibrium back,

took a couple of deep breaths and hoped my face had gone back to its usual colour. I also tried real hard not to look too guilty. Big mistake, because (a) my Mom knows each and every expression I own, and interprets them like an expert lie-detector, and (b) I forgot I hadn't gone in either of the doors, so Mom didn't know I was in the house.

She stared at me. 'Catrin? I didn't know you were home! Why didn't you say so?'

'Oh, hi, Mom.' I racked my brains for something un-incriminating to say. 'I guess you were too busy listening to the Beach Boys to hear me call.'

You'll notice I didn't exactly *say* I called. I just said she wouldn't have heard me if I had, which I hadn't. Mom's eyes narrowed suspiciously, so I gave what I hoped was a real nonchalant grin and beetled off.

Dad was talking to someone in the living room, so he and Walt (oh, Walt, please don't be the Spoiler!) had brought someone else home.

The person's back was towards me, but Dad saw me come in. 'Hi, honeybun, didn't know you were home, Mom didn't say.'

'Mom didn't hear me come in,' I said, truthfully. The person turned round. He was very handsome, and quite young – only a couple of years older than me from the look of him.

'Honey, this is Brett. He's a graduate trainee – he just graduated from Oxford, and he's gonna be working for me now.'

My ex-friend Kymburleigh would have positively

drooled. He was *gorgeous*! Thick, dark lashes over light blue eyes, brown skin, real good teeth, tall, handsome . . . I put out my hand to shake his, feeling a silly grin creeping onto my face. Dad was watching me with an amused expression.

Then our hands touched and everything changed. I went first hot, then cold, and it wasn't, trust me on this, passion, unrequited or otherwise. *He was, without any doubt, the fourth Spoiler.*

'Hi!' he said. 'Your Dad didn't say he had such a gorgeous daughter!'

Creep! I thought, *Rat Fink!* I thought, *Dolphin murderer!* I thought. But I didn't say any of those things. I sort of Scarlett O'Hara'd him to death. 'Why, you're so kind!' I simpered, carefully and thankfully withdrawing my hand. 'It's real good to have you here! Welcome!' (*Liar, liar, pants on fire!* I thought). I heard Walt come in the room behind me and swung round. 'Oh, hi, Walt!' I burbled, hoping frantically that he wouldn't say a thing about me trespassing in his room.

He didn't. 'Hi, Catrin,' he replied, his face sober. 'What have you been doing with yourself today?'

'Oh, just hanging out with Twm, I guess,' I said, thinking, *and tracking down Spoilers, and listening to their plans, and rescuing the Sea Girl, and finding the Signs. Oh, and discovering the identity of the fourth Spoiler who is now INSIDE the Toll House.*

It turned out that Dad had invited Brett to eat dinner with us. He was staying in a bed and breakfast in Pontpentre-dŵr, and would be travelling to and from the factory with Dad and Walt. Which meant, knowing Dad, that Brett would be invited home to eat more often than not, and Mom wouldn't object. She always loved to feed folks, especially young male folks who would appreciate her chocolate fudge brownies and pot roasts.

So we all sat down to eat together. Jake was still off with Cei and Rhodri – looked like he was set for the entire school vacation, so it meant I had to be all grown-up and eat with the damn Spoiler. I made sure I was sitting between Dad and Walt. I didn't want a Spoiler any closer to me than I could help, but that meant I was looking right at his horrible, handsome face. He was good, I'll give him that. He made polite small talk with Mom and Dad, and funned around with me a whole lot. It was real hard to joke back at him. I noticed he didn't have much to say to Walt, however, and that made me glad. I *knew* all along the Spoiler couldn't be Walt, I just knew it.

After dinner, everybody was settling down to drink coffee, and I didn't think I could stand much more of being polite to that cuckoo in our family nest. I excused myself, unhooked Madoc's leash from the back of the kitchen door and let him out of the outhouse, where Mom had shut him because of Brett visiting. I was bending down, clipping the leash to his collar, when I heard the kitchen door open and close behind me. I swung round, and thank goodness it was Walt.

'Catty, do you mind some company while you walk Madoc?' he asked. 'Don't feel you have to say yes – I know it's good to be alone sometimes.'

'Oh, Walt, yeah. Please come. I guess we need to talk.'

Walt grinned, his teeth white and even in the red-brown skin. 'Yeah, I guess we do.'

The air was cool and slightly damp after a brief shower earlier in the evening. I could smell the sea, and there was the other after-rain smell of grass and trees and stuff that is always so gorgeous.

We didn't talk for a while, not until we were well clear of the Toll House, and strolling along the edge of the incoming tide, luminous and frothy in the moonlight. I let Madoc off the leash and he rushed about sticking his nose into every pile of seaweed, every rock pool and every crevice he came to, his plumy tail thrashing madly with delight.

'Walt,' I said at last. 'I need to tell you some stuff.'

CHAPTER SEVENTEEN

Walt didn't speak at all while I told him what had been going on, beginning with the Spoilers' first attempt to wreck the coastline of Wales, and ending up with the Sea Girl, and the day's adventures.

'I know it sounds real hard to believe, Walt, but all of it's true, I swear it is, every single word.' I had to make him believe me, but it was easier than I'd thought.

'Oh, I believe you,' he said, picking up a flat pebble and skimming it out across the incoming tide. 'Mrs Takahashi already told me some of that stuff before I came over, and we – you and Twm and I – have a whole lot in common, Catrin. In my tribe I'm what's called a Shaman. Know what that is?'

'Yeah. Kind of. It's, like, a wise man, isn't it? A medicine man.'

'Yes, in its simplest sense, I guess. I'm responsible for the harmony of my people and the land they live in. I have to try to keep the balance between our needs and those of nature. Sometimes it's real hard, when tribes decide they want to open a gambling casino on tribal lands, but there's usually some way round it that won't upset the Spirits too much. When all's said and done, these are modern times, and a man – even a Native American – needs to adapt to survive! I guess I'm lucky, because they still mostly consult me before they do stuff. In some tribes, they don't bother, and that's real bad medicine. But I knew Twm for a shaman when I first touched his hand, and I'm pretty sure he recognised me, the same way.'

'Oh, he did, he really did. He said it felt like an electric shock when you touched. Look, Walt, I really, really want to apologise for snooping in your room and all, but when we overheard the Spoilers say they had someone already in the Toll House, well, you were the only one we could think of. But now – '

'I know,' he said grimly, 'Brett.'

'Yeah. It's a major bummer, because now Mom's met him, she'll want to keep feeding him. My Mom's like that. She once helped run a soup kitchen in Pittsburgh, and we all had to go feed the street people on Thanksgiving. I hated it. It felt so dumb – like the Christmas scene from *Little Women* or something!'

Walt laughed. 'Louisa May Alcott has a whole lot to answer for, I guess. All the same, I imagine the street people appreciated it.'

'Maybe. I'm not so sure they did. Some of the guys cursed at me.'

'People are like that. Don't like to be beholden to people. All to do with pride, and even down-and-outs have pride sometimes.'

'I guess. But what are we gonna do about Brett?'

'Do? Absolutely nothing. We know who he is, now, and we can keep our eyes on him, so we've kind of managed to neutralise him. If we hadn't known, then he might have been dangerous. But now we do, so we can fix him if he needs to be fixed.'

'I like the sound of that. Can we fix him permanently?'

'Not the way you mean. But we can certainly make sure he can't do us – or the dolphins and seals – any harm.'

'That reminds me. Twm's looking for the dolphins now. We overheard the Spoilers say they were gonna try and beach them again. Well, not in so many words, but that's what they meant, I guess. I wish there was something we could do to scare the Spoilers off. I'd hate it if the dolphins were harmed.'

Walt grinned, and his eyes flashed wickedness. 'Oh, I think there may be something we can do. Think we can get Madoc back inside the Toll House without being caught?'

I nodded.

'Come on, then. Race you.'

I half tripped, turning to run, and Madoc bounced round me excitedly. Walt was way ahead, but by the time we reached the edge of the beach, I'd almost caught up, although his legs were twice as long as mine. I guess he let me catch up. Adults do that, don't they, and I wish they wouldn't. Kids don't mind losing sometimes! Back at the house I put my hand round Madoc's muzzle to silence him, and opened the door of the outhouse to put him inside. He looked at me real reproachfully, but it cut no ice with me at all. 'I'll be back soon, boy,' I whispered. 'Stay quiet, OK?'

Back on the beach, Walt grasped my shoulders. 'Look, Catrin, I'm going to show you something I've never shown another human being – except my Grandpa, who taught me how to do it. It might be a bit scary, but keep your cool, OK?'

I nodded, cautiously. I wasn't quite sure what he was gonna do. Excitement caught at my breath. Walt stepped back, and raised both arms to the sky. He started chanting some words – in Iroquois, I guess – and began turning in a slow circle on the spot. As he came round again to face me, I realised that his outline was blurring. He seemed to be shrinking. His arms seemed to be changing shape. I guess I stopped breathing, because before my eyes Walt shimmered and changed. Instead of a six-foot-plus Native American, there was a large and fierce-looking owl . . .

It flexed its powerful wings and opened its beak. Fierce golden eyes glared at me.

'W-Walt?' I asked.

I heard his voice in my head, not my ears. 'Don't be afraid. This is me. Remember my native name, Catrin. I'm gonna go and try to find the Spoilers. Maybe show them the error of their ways a little.' He bent his legs and flapped his wings and took off. I watched enviously as he circled above me.

Suddenly I remembered I had a packet of Taid's fairy dust in the pocket of my jeans. I whipped it out, ripped it open, and thinking *owl, owl, owl*, I shut my eyes and hoped.

Oooo! To-whit-to-whoooooops! I tried to walk and tripped over my feet, spread my arms – wings – to balance myself and landed on my beak. I finally got the hang of standing up at least. I flapped my wings and shot upwards, cannoning into Walt, who hooted with amusement.

'You're using your wings wrong,' he explained in owl talk, 'you need to kind of row, not flap. Like you're in a boat and rowing rather than flapping up and down like you're trying to fold a bedsheet!'

Eventually I got the hang of it, and wing-tip to wing-tip, we went looking.

We searched along the coast, and finally found them on the beach at Penbryn. Miss Critchett and Dewi were standing at the edge of the tide, where the little river flowed into the sea, and they had a large battery-operated ghetto blaster with them. The unmistakable sound of a dolphin's distress call echoed from the tape across the beach, and I searched the moonlit sea frantically, hoping against hope that I wouldn't see a family of arched, silvery backs heading inshore.

The horizon was clear, so maybe Twm had gotten to the dolphins first. The Spoilers turned up the volume on the boom box. 'Why aren't they coming?' Mordreda Critchett muttered crossly. 'Every dolphin within earshot should be heading inshore right now. We should have half a dozen of them thrashing about in the sand.'

'Maybe you've already scared them off. Maybe now we can go ahead with the oil survey,' Dewi said, lighting a cigarette. 'Anyway, I'm getting bored. I'm going down the pub.'

'Oh no, you aren't,' Mordreda hissed. 'You are going to get your boat and take me out. There's still the seals and the puffins and the shearwaters and anything else that lives out there that can stop us getting permission to prospect for the oil. So you can forget the pub.'

'But my boat's miles away.' Dewi protested.

'Then we'll get in the car and go there.' Mordreda Critchett turned and began to stalk up the beach, stumbling slightly on the large round stones at the beachhead. 'Come on,' she ordered, and Dewi flipped his cigarette butt into the sea, picked up the tape machine and followed her.

Walt flew up from his perch on the rocks beneath the cliffs. They hadn't noticed us. Their car was parked in the turning circle beside the river, and Walt overtook them, and perched on their car like a giant hood ornament, facing the windscreen. Because it was dark, they got in the car without noticing him, and it was only when Dewi turned on the headlights that they saw him, outlined against the beam.

'Aaargh!' Dewi shrieked. 'What is it?'

'It's only an owl, stupid,' Mordreda sighed. 'Start the car. It will soon shift itself. Or it might fall off and you can squash it.'

Dewi shakily put the car into gear and moved off, but Walt stayed put, staring fixedly through the glass at the driver. I flapped along overhead for a bit, out of sight of the passengers in the car, and then decided it was wasted effort on my part, and perched instead on the car roof while Dewi drove up the hill from the beach. Not quite as easy as it sounds, because my talons couldn't grip the shiny paintwork. In the end I hung on to the radio aerial in the middle with both feet. Walt clung on to the silvery ornament on the hood, and I wondered what his plan was.

I soon found out. He took off, circled, and his owl-shape suddenly blurred with speed as he dive-bombed the car, veering away at the last minute so the car swerved crazily. He did it again and again, until the car skidded crazily from side to side, bounced off the bank on the left, and then shot across the road – and over the edge. Fortunately – or un-, depending on a person's point of view about the Spoilers – the car was at a place that was thickly wooded, otherwise it probably would have bounced all the way down to the bottom of the valley and into the river. As it was it just went down about two metres, slammed into a tree, and stopped, steam hissing from the bonnet.

With a squawk of alarm, I shot off the roof as the car left the road, and was relieved to see Walt spring into the air, and perch in the tree. I joined him and we watched as the car doors opened and two groggy occupants clambered out and back on to the road.

Dewi had hit his nose on the steering wheel, and blood gushed down his front, while Mordreda Critchett had a lump the size of an egg on her forehead. I guess maybe they hadn't been wearing seat-belts.

'You stupid fool!' she shrieked. 'Look what you've done to Mrs Gwynne Davies's beautiful car!'

'Wasn't my fault!' Dewi groaned. 'There was a monster with huge, glowing eyes dive-bombing us'

'It was only an owl, that's all! Perhaps if you drank

162

less, you wouldn't hallucinate! Now, get that car back on the road.'

'How do you suggest I do that, then?'

'Well, I don't know! You're a man, aren't you? Men are supposed to be good at that sort of thing.'

'What, hauling half a ton of car up a bank? Maybe Superman. Not me, lady. Dream on.'

'Then what do you propose we do?'

Dewi scratched his head. 'Walk?'

'Walk where, for heaven's sake?'

'How about up the hill, onto the road, and flag down a car? Or find a phone and call a taxi, I don't mind.'

Mordreda fumbled in her handbag. 'I've got a mobile. I'll phone one from here. I can't possibly walk all that way in these shoes!'

Dewi grinned. 'Mobile? You can try, Mordreda. But you won't get a signal, not down here.'

He was right. There was nothing else for it but for them to walk. They set off into the darkness, bickering away, Mordreda's whiny voice getting fainter and fainter as they disappeared.

'What now, Walt?' I asked.

'How about we try and find Twm?' he suggested.

Seemed like a good idea to me.

CHAPTER EIGHTEEN

I was pretty sure that Twm would be at sea someplace – under it, not on it. We flew back to the shore and I gave myself a shake to get myself out from under Taid's powder and back to normal. It had been a weird experience being a bird – I didn't think I'd repeat it in too much of a hurry, though! Getting back to normal made me feel kinda nauseous. Walt's outline blurred and wavered, and soon the owl was gone and he was back.

'Not a lot of what I do can startle you, I guess,' he said, picking a stray feather out of my hair, 'you knowing Twm's Taid and all.'

'Not really. I'm getting quite blasé about magic! Question, is, where's Twm? He's probably out there someplace,' I said, gesturing out to sea and answering my own question. 'I'll swim out and go find him.'

'Count me out,' Walt said, shuddering. 'I can't follow you there.'

'Is it just birds you can do then?' I asked, curious to know how far his strange powers went.

'Yeah. I learned I could do this when I was just a kid. There I was, meditating with my Grandpa in the *kiva,* thinking dreams, and next thing I knew I was half a mile up in the air, looking down on it. You know what a *kiva* is?'

'It's a quiet place, right? Like a sweat lodge?'

'You got it. I kind of travelled out of my head and learned I could stay there – and take bird shapes while I was at it. Trouble is, changing back gets more and more difficult as I get older. My body likes to stay birdshape. I may not be able to do it much longer. Or I may have to decide to be one shape or another. And I guess my wife and kids might complain if I picked bird!'

'That's the first time I ever did anything like that. I couldn't have done it without Taid's powder –'

'I must get to meet this Taid.'

'I'm sure you will, real soon. Anyhow, Walt, I'm gonna go find Twm.'

'Take care. I'll wait for you.'

I kicked off my shoes and stripped down to my t-shirt and pants, leaving my jeans and sweatshirt with Walt. Then I waded out, and ducked down under the waves. The water was freezing, but I knew that as soon as I began to breathe it, I'd be warm again.

I stroked out in the dark water, kicking just under the surface. I steeled myself to take my first breath – it was kinda like that first in-breath a person takes using a snorkel – you're never quite sure if you're gonna get a lungful of water from it, even if you blow to clear it first! But the water entering my lungs didn't harm me any. I just pootled along breathing happily. My eyesight adjusted to underwater: there wasn't a whole lot of light down there, but I could still see clearly. I swam out a couple of hundred yards, and ran into a half-dozen grey seals.

'Hey!' I greeted them, and they swam curiously

around me. One of them nudged me with his nose, and I looked into interested black eyes. 'You guys seen Twm?' I asked, and they seemed to understand, because the whole lot turned and swam out to sea. I tagged along, but when I began to trail behind, the biggest one came back and waggled his hind flippers in my face. I took the offer and hung on. He towed me behind him, my hair streaming back from my face, as he arrowed through the water. After a while, I saw the graceful shapes of a dolphin family ahead, and spotted Twm in the centre of them. He had an arm around the smallest, and was scratching it under its smiling mouth while he talked. The seals joined the group, and looped around and under the great, silvery mammals.

I swam to Twm's side and butted noses with the baby dolphin. Mama dolphin nudged me gently, and I turned and butted noses with her, too.

'You got the message across I guess, Twm?'

He nodded. 'I got here just in time. The Spoilers were playing the damn distress call, and all the dolphins within range were heading for the sands ready to beach themselves.'

'How did you stop them?'

'I got them singing. That way they drowned out the false call with their own calls. If they can't hear it, they can't respond to it. But it was hard. I think the Spoilers have something else up their sleeves.'

'Oh, no. What?

'They netted a seal a week or so back, kept it overnight and then just released it. When it got back I couldn't see anything on it, like a scar where a microchip might have been fitted, or a tracking device, something like that, but the dolphins tell me that in the last couple of days it's been out of sorts.'

'Out of sorts. You mean, like, ill?'

'Yes. I've got this horrible feeling they might have infected it with the seal virus – PDV it's called – and then turned it loose. Of course as soon as they released it, it headed straight back to the colony. So if that's what they've done, they might've infected the whole lot. The virus is a killer if it isn't treated. Once all the seals are dead the Spoilers will have one less obstacle in the way of their oil exploration. That only leaves the dolphins and the island birds.'

I stared at him, horrified. 'Oh, Twm, no! What can we do?'

'There's a vaccine that works, but it probably costs a lot of money – and how can we get the seals vaccinated – no one's going to just do it on our say-so, are they?'

I felt better, suddenly. 'Oh, come on, Twm! Have you forgotten the Signs?'

His face cleared. 'The Sea Harp and the Sky Egg! Of course! If we can get at a vet, we can get them immunised right away!'

'So what are we waiting for?'

We left the dolphins with firm instructions not to answer any distress or Seaname calls without investigating them first to make sure they were genuine. We reassured the seals that we weren't gonna leave them to die, told them to gather their clans and all of them head for Skomer, and just wait. We'd meet them there with veterinarians who would immunise them all against the virus. There were still so many problems to overcome, but at least we were able to help them now, we weren't just sitting waiting for something to happen, and in a weird way that felt real good, you know?

We waded ashore, and Walt was waiting with my dry clothes. I disappeared into the shadows to take off my wet t-shirt and underpants and dressed in my jeans and sweatshirt. Walt headed back to the Toll House, and as soon as he'd gone, Twm and I headed for Taid's cave to get the Signs.

Taid was rocking quietly in his chair, smoking a sweet-smelling pipe. He heaved himself out of his chair and retrieved the three Signs from the place he'd hidden them. He handed the Sky Egg and the Sea Harp to me. The heavy Earthstone in its iron chest he gave to Twm. 'You carry that, boy. Too heavy for my girl, it is.'

'Aw, shucks, Taid. Little ol', helpless, dainty me!' I chortled, doing my best Southern Belle impression. Twm aimed a pretend clout at my ear and I ducked away. I tucked the two Signs I was to carry into my backpack. The Sky Egg's protective box was coated in a thin film of ice.

Taid handed us further supplies of his fairy dust and we disappeared in the general direction of Cardigan town centre, arriving in a rush in the first empty dawn-pink street we spotted. No point in spreading alarm amongst the natives, right?

The RSPCA offices were in a kind of storefront in the Inspector's house. We rang the doorbell, but there was no reply. Twm rang it again, and at last the curtains in the room above were drawn back, the window was flung open, and a becurlered head stuck out.

'Who's that?'

'It's Twm, Mrs Price. We need to see the Inspector, urgently,' Twm called up. 'Sorry to disturb you, but it's an emergency.'

'I'll wake him. He won't be pleased, mind. He was out on the islands until the early hours. Something's up with the bird colonies.' The head withdrew, and Twm and I exchanged worried glances.

'Oh, no, don't say the Spoilers have got to the birds already!' Twm fretted.

There was the sound of a door being unbolted, and a stocky dark man in a tartan dressing gown, his hair sticking up all over, stood back to let us in.

'Should have known it was you, young Twm!' he yawned. 'Could have done with you last night on Skomer. The RSPB and us have been out there since early afternoon. Terrible, it is.'

'What happened?' Twm asked, tense as a bowstring with worry.

'Some sadistic swine has released a pack of ferrets onto the island, and dumped a couple of barrels of oil in the water offshore. Looked like used chip-fat, but it's just as bad as a slick of crude oil when it gets in their feathers. We've lost a lot of shearwaters and puffins, and birds of a good few other species, besides. I've left men out there trying to trap the ferrets, but the birds started to leave their nests – and their young – as soon as the sun came up, and some of them headed straight into the sea and got oiled up. The breeding colonies aren't going to be worth a damn this year. I reckon eighty per cent of the parent birds have flown. We won't get them back unless there's a miracle.'

Twm and I stared at each other, aghast. The Spoilers had beaten us to the birds after all!

'So, young Twm,' Mr Price said, plopping down on a waiting room chair and squinting blearily at us. 'Since I only just got to bed, and I haven't been so tired since Wales beat England 31-30 and I stayed up all night celebrating, it had better be something important.'

'It is, Mr Price. We need to get the vet out, straight away. I've found a seal showing signs of PDV. Runny eyes, coughing, classic symptoms, like last time in '98.'

Mr Price's mouth opened and shut. 'As if we didn't have enough on our plates with the birds! Oh, *Duw.* That virus is a killer if we don't get to it fast enough. Well, nothing else for it. I'd better put on my wellies and phone Iorrie Cow-killer to come and have a look. Hope you're wrong, though, boy. Maybe it's just got a cold or something.'

'*Iorrie Cow-killer?*' I whispered faintly, as Mr Price headed upstairs to dress. 'Iorrie Cow-Killer is a veterinarian?'

Twm grinned faintly. 'Goes back to his first week

170

in practice, Catrin, just out of college. According to a local farmer he killed two of his cows on his first visit. They would have died anyway, according to Iorrie, but he got the blame, unfortunately. Unforgiving lot, Cardi farmers!'

'Do you think the Spoilers released the ferrets on the islands?' I asked, getting back to the subject.

'Who else? At least Mr Price is giving us the benefit of the doubt about the PDV, but I don't expect Iorrie will. He's the type who doesn't believe in anything unless you shove it right up his nose.'

'But if they're sick, he'll see for himself, won't he?'

'Unlikely. They won't all be sick yet. What he'll see is a colony of healthy seals. The sick ones, if we're right about it, will hide away from him. It's what sick creatures do, hole up somewhere quiet until they get better – or die. So I imagine we'll have to use the signs to convince him.'

'At least we won't need the Earthstone this time!' I said, and grinned, remembering how we'd used it to break out of a storecupboard by turning the wooden shelves and back wall into a living forest.

'Hope not. But you never know.'

CHAPTER NINETEEN

Iorrie Cow-killer, a tiny leprechaun of a man with a brown, sun-wrinkled face and fierce eyes, met us at Martins Haven, where a yawning boatman rooted from his bed by Mr Price's phone call, waited at the jetty to take us out to Skomer. The vet had a big black case with him that he assured us was stuffed with PDV vaccine, just in case.

'Morning, Iorrie.'

'Morning, Dai.'

'Thought I'd seen the last of this place for a couple of hours,' Mr Price grumbled, 'and here I am back again. Hope it's not a wild goose chase, my boy. I hope you're wrong.'

'Unfortunately, I don't think I am,' Twm said. I clutched the Signs, knowing that it wouldn't be – at least as far as Mr Price and Iorrie would know.

The little boat chugged out on the sunlit sea. As we got closer to the island we saw traces of cold, greasy oil floating, and here and there oiled birds struggled to rise out of the water at our approach, failing miserably.

Iorrie and Mr Price hauled in every one they could reach. By the time the boat nosed into the little landing stage, the bottom of the boat was filled with frightened, struggling seabirds: manx shearwaters, puffins, fulmars, storm petrels. Anger nearly choked me; I was so furious that if I'd met a Spoiler right that minute I'd probably have punched him or her right on the nose.

The boatman held the boat close to the jetty while we clambered off. 'I'll take these back to the volunteer washers at the sea bird centre,' he suggested, 'and come back for you after, all right?'

Iorrie Cow-killer nodded, and led the way up the rocky cliffside towards the seal colonies on the far side of the island.

It looked like every seal in Cardigan Bay had obeyed Twm's instructions: the inlets and bays were thick with black, wriggling, liquid-eyed creatures, barking and flopping and rolling. Some of them were the new season's pups, and I felt my face split into a dumb grin at the sight of them. How people can look one of those little guys in the eye and smash its skull with a club, or shoot it, is beyond me.

'Look healthy enough to me,' Iorrie muttered crossly. 'If they're sickening for something it doesn't show. Sure you aren't mistaken, Twm?'

'Positive,' Twm said. 'Show them, Catrin!'

The two men stared at me, mystified, as I opened my backpack, drew out the Sea Harp and passed it to Twm. He ran his long fingers over the strings, and the liquid, exquisite sound made their eyes glaze over real good. In the meantime, I had taken out the icy Sky Egg, and was holding it in both hands, the cold making my fingers ache horribly.

'Look,' I said, nodding at a perfectly healthy-looking seal. 'That one's got all the symptoms! Its eyes are running, and so is its nose. It's definitely got the virus, hasn't it?' Then Twm ran his fingers over the Harp again, to unfreeze them.

Iorrie Cow-killer crouched down beside the creature, which tried to wriggle healthily away. A word from Twm stilled it, and it lay quiet while Iorrie took its temperature – which was probably perfectly normal – and pronounced the seal very sick indeed. That's the thing about the Sea Harp and the Sky Egg – the Harp freezes them still as stone, the Sea Egg makes them believe anything I tell 'em . . .

'We need to immunise the whole colony,' he decided. 'Dai, you and Twm take some of the syringes – they're single dose syrettes, so put them in a disposal bag when you've used them – and start injecting as many as will let you.' He turned to me. 'What about you, lovely girl? You think you can help?'

'Of course I can!' I said indignantly, shoving the Sky Egg back in its box and into the backpack. 'Just show me how.'

Iorrie showed me how to jab the needle into the seal's body, press the plunger and withdraw it, watched me do a couple of seals, and grinned.

'Natural, you are,' he said, handing me a box. 'Off you go, now.'

Between us we immunised a couple of hundred perfectly healthy-looking seals. Some of them barked indignantly at us, and one or two of the babies got big, fat tears rolling down their faces, which made me feel real bad, but I kept on reassuring them that it was

174

for their own good, so they didn't get sick, and I think they understood. Twm was talking to them in their own language, and I decided he was gonna have to teach me that, and quick.

At last, we stood up and flexed our aching backs. As we'd treated each seal, they flopped away and into the water. The only seal left was one that really did look sick. Twm went over to it and put his hand on its head.

'I think we need to take this one back,' he said. 'He looks sicker than the others did.'

Way sicker, since the others looked perfectly healthy to everyone but Iorrie and Dai Price! No matter: they had a sick seal to prove the virus was there!

Iorrie and Dai loaded the seal into a sturdy cage and carried it down to the jetty where the Martins Haven boatman was waiting for us. He had another boatload of oiled birds, but the oil seemed to be dispersing, so with luck the worst was over. A couple of drums of oil is a minor spill compared to what happened when the *Sea Empress* hit the rocks at Milford Haven. All the same I got that 'wanna thump a Spoiler' feeling again!

Iorrie Cow-killer gave us a lift back to Pontpentre-dŵr and headed off to the seal rescue centre with his precious cargo. Dai Price and his final load of oiled birds went back to the bird rescue hospital, ready to raise the troops to go find any stragglers that might have made it to shore. As Iorrie's car disappeared down the lane, Twm and I gave each other a high-five.

'We did it!' I crowed. 'We beat the Spoilers!'

'For the time being,' Twm said, soberly. 'But they're still here, and I don't think they'll give up this easily.'

'I better get back home,' I decided. 'I haven't seen Mom or Dad since yesterday, and I guess I'd better touch base with them. By the way, I'm all out of Taid's powder – you think he's got any more?'

'Of course he has. In his cave he has all sorts of stuff. I'll get some. I just want to check on Cei, make sure he's all right with Rhodri for a bit longer. I'll tell Rhodri's Mam that Taid is away for a rest – which is true. I'm sure she'll keep him until all this is over.'

Back at the Toll House, Walt and Dad were out walking, so only Mom was in. She wasn't baking, although the lingering smell proved she had been, quite recently. I could also smell roast chicken, I hoped for lunch. I was starving after my adventures of the morning, and fairly exhausted after being up most of the night, too. Mom was up in her studio, bear-making.

'Hi, Mom!' I said, sticking my head round the door. 'Can I come in?' I always ask, because the studio is her quiet place, and every so often she likes to shut herself away and think some, and then she doesn't want even Dad or me or Jake in there.

'Oh, hi, honeybun.' She looked up, then put her head on one side to survey the ear-less, eye-less bear she was stitching. 'What kind of face should this one have? Cheeky? Stern?'

'Oh, you can't have a stern bear, Mom, unless you make it a school-teacher,' I joked.

'Oh, that's a brilliant idea, Catty!' she crowed, reaching for an ear. 'I can make a little tiny mortarboard from felt, and make a black gown to go with it. Oh, he's gonna be so cute!'

Madoc was downstairs shrieking to be let in to lick me seven ways from Sunday, so I went and opened the door. I was on my knees rubbing his ears and scratching his chest and making good dog noises when the dragonhead doorknocker crashed down, scaring me stiff. Madoc stopped leaping at me and leapt for the front door instead, hurtling himself at it, braking at the last minute and skidding along, barking frantically with excitement, across the quarry tiles on an accumulation of rag rugs.

However, once he reached the door and pressed his nose to the gap at the bottom, the hair on the back of his neck rose, and he began to growl. His ears and tail went down, and his lips drew back, showing his teeth. I grabbed his collar, wondering why he was behaving that way, but when I opened the door, I knew.

Madoc snarled louder, the whites of his eyes showing, and I felt pretty much like doing the same. It was Brett the Spoiler, all gussied up in spotless cream chinos and a rolled-sleeve black shirt. He flashed perfect teeth at me, and twinkled bluely behind his dark lashes. I wanted to spit in his eye, I was so mad.

I began to say, 'What do you want?' but stopped myself just in time. I didn't want him to guess I was on to him, did I? So I remembered my one-time best chum back in Pittsburgh, and did a Kymburleigh . . .

'Oh, *hi Brett*!' I warbled. 'Oh, it's *sooo good* to *see* you again! Did my Mom invite you to Sunday lunch?'

His smile wobbled a bit, and the blue eyes narrowed slightly. 'Yeah, she did. Hope that's OK with you?'

'Oh, hey, of course it is! That's like, so cool! Mom's in her studio. I'll just give her a call, tell her you're here.' I didn't intend to invite him in – that was one thing I'd learned the last time, never formally invite a Spoiler into the home – it gives them powers they wouldn't otherwise have. I wrestled the still snarling Madoc into the outhouse and gave him a doggybik and a promise that some day soon he could bite Brett as hard as he liked. He grunted and started to snarf down the bone-shaped biscuit. I shut the door and turned, to find Brett standing just behind me. My smile slipped a bit, but no matter, I pasted it back on real quick. And he was inside without being invited, which was good. Round one to me!

'Mom!' I hollered up the stairs. 'Brett's here! How come you didn't tell me you asked him to lunch? I would have put on a dress instead of these scuzzy old Levis!'

Brett looked smug at that. Maybe he thought I was, like, flirting with him or something! Mom scuttled downstairs, a matchmaking gleam in her eye. How come she didn't get it when Twm was around, huh? How come this graduate trainee got it and Twm didn't? All the same, I knew she liked Twm. So why? I decided I was gonna have to have a Mom and daughter heart-to-heart some day soon.

'Good to see you, Brett! Lunch won't be long. Come through into the rose garden. Catty honey, will you bring our guest a drink?'

'Sure, Mom, no problem!' I gushed right back with my sweetest smile. *What would you like, Brett-the-Spoiler*, I thought, *cyanide julep, arsenic cocktail?*

In the fridge I found a pitcher of Mom's iced tea with lemon, which is always good on a hot day. I fixed three glasses with ice and sprigs of mint and put them on a tray to take outside. Mom was sitting in the glider under the canopy, and Brett was perched beside her on the grass.

'Catty,' Mom said, taking her glass from the tray, 'Brett was just remarking that if he'd known what a gorgeous daughter I have, he'd have pestered your Dad for a visit long before now.'

'She takes after her mother, Mrs Morgan,' Brett sighed.

Ooh, I wanted to kick him so hard! But here he was, in my home, and I was gonna have to deal with him somehow. The worst thing I could do would be to forget for one second that he was a Spoiler, and dangerous.

CHAPTER TWENTY

He kept up the flirtatious banter right through lunch, but that didn't stop him devouring every scrap Mom put in front of him. Walt and Dad came back in good time to eat, so at least I had an ally there at table with me.

Walt was great – he kept asking Brett questions he didn't know the answers to about the Takahashi Corporation – as a graduate trainee I guess maybe he should have read up on the company, but he obviously hadn't. At first I wasn't real sure what he was trying to do, but then I realised that he was working at keeping Brett unsettled – he was less likely to learn anything or do anything that way. What made it even funnier was that Brett was being terribly English, and talking to Walt like he was a stone-age half-wit instead of a guy with a PhD who just happened to be a Native American! I guess the braids and dream-catcher fooled him.

After lunch we took coffee into the garden, and while we were drinking it – me still sitting as far away from Brett as I could get without actually being out of the garden entirely – Jake came home.

Being Jake, he was more interested in seeing Madoc than being polite to company, and as a result Madoc got let out of the outhouse and came hurtling into the garden to see us all. Naturally he took offence at seeing Brett on the premises, and before anyone could stop him, he sank his teeth into Brett's immaculate chinos . . .

Mom screeched, and Dad hauled Madoc off and locked him up again in disgrace, and Brett clutched his calf and tried not to show how much it must have hurt. I sent out a telepathic message to Madoc that he'd get goodies for that, just as soon as I could smuggle them to him!

Mom inspected the bluish dents on the hairy leg. 'Didn't break the skin, Brett, thank heavens, so no need for tetanus shots. I can't apologise enough. What's gotten into that dog? He doesn't normally attack people.'

'Not people he likes, anyhow,' Jake said. 'Maybe Madoc has rabies, Mom.'

Looked like Jake wasn't any too keen on our guest, either.

'I'll take these indoors and load the dishwasher,' I said, picking up the tray of coffee cups. Anything to get away from that damn Spoiler squatting like a malevolent toad in our backyard!

Inside, the house was cool, and I puttered about scraping plates into the waste bin, and loading crockery into the machine. I lifted the drop down door up and clicked it into place when suddenly a pair of arms wrapped round my waist from behind.

Whoa! I thought, realising instantly that these were not my Dad's arms, Walt was much too much of a gentleman to do it, and they certainly weren't Jake's. If Jake had hugged me I'd have sent for the doctor, right off! No, these arms were indubitably Brett's, and my response was instinctive. I swung round, hauled off and slugged him one, right on the chin.

OK, OK, not very ladylike, that I'll admit, but it sure put him off, because his eyes crossed and he slithered to the kitchen floor, unconscious. I tucked my aching knuckles under my armpit and wondered what on earth I was gonna do now. I never knew I packed a punch like that! But then, I'd never slugged anyone before. But I had a funny idea Mom and Dad were not about to be real impressed by an unconscious house guest . . .

Fortunately, the next person into the kitchen was Walt.

'Catty! What happened?'

'He made a pass, and so I hauled off and slugged him. What am I gonna do, Walt?'

'Well, when he comes round, what we need to do is convince him he tripped and maybe hit his head.'

'He's not gonna believe that, is he?' Unless . . . A grin spread over my face. I still had the Sea Harp and the Sky Egg in my backpack upstairs. 'I just need to get something. Try not to let anybody see him until I come back, OK?'

Walt, mystified, nodded, bending over the just-stirring figure on the floor.

I shot upstairs, got the Signs and hurtled down again. I got back just as Brett was starting to sit up, holding his jaw and looking bemused. Well, he was gonna look a whole lot more bemused by the time I'd finished with him!

'Put your fingers in your ears, Walt!' I instructed, and he obeyed without asking questions. I held the Sea Harp and ran my fingers across the strings. It didn't sound quite as good as when Twm did it, but it did the trick all the same. Brett's eyes glazed even more, and he froze, half-sitting up, half lying down. I put down the shell – I saw his eyes follow it, so he knew exactly what it was – and took the Sky Egg from its box.

'Now, Brett,' I said, trying not to grin. 'You will believe everything I tell you, forever and a day. First off, you are not a Spoiler. You are a good guy, and whatever the Spoilers tell you to do, you'll do the opposite. Right?'

He stared. That was all he could do. Walt did, too, for different reasons.

'Right. Second, you will resign from Takahashi International as soon as you humanly can. No one will talk you out of this.'

Blank stare.

'Good. Third, you will do everything in your power to protect wildlife in Cardigan Bay and everywhere else in the world. In fact, you'll go work for Save Our Sea Shores, World Wide Fund for Nature, Greenpeace, something like that – uh – shadowing illegal whaling boats, tracking nuclear waste, fast as you can. OK?'

Blank stare.

'And lastly, you will forget everything that just happened. You didn't make a pass at me, and I certainly didn't slug you. Right?'

Stare.

I put down the Sky Egg and picked up the Sea Harp. A brief tinkle on the strings and – hey presto – Brett was back with us.

'Ow! My jaw hurts. What happened?'

Walt jumped in to save me lying, I guess. 'Not a clue. I came in and found you flat on your back. Maybe you fainted from the shock of Madoc biting you. I guess you should pay a visit to the emergency room. Maybe get some tetanus shots after all. What do you think, Catrin?'

'Shots would be good. How do you feel, Brett?'

'A bit light-headed, but that's all. I'm all right, I think. I don't need to go to hospital. I think maybe I need to go back to my flat and rest a while.'

'I think that's a real good plan,' I said, smiling sweetly.

'And I need to see Mr Morgan tomorrow, first thing,' Brett said, a puzzled expression on his face. 'I don't think a career with Takahashi is really for me. I've got this feeling I need to do something different.'

'Oh, I'm real sad to hear that,' Walt said, pokerfaced. 'What did you have in mind?'

'Something in conservation. Maybe –'

'Save our Sea Shores? Greenpeace?' I suggested, sweetly.

'Brilliant idea!' he said. 'See you tomorrow, Walt.'

And he was gone.

Walt and I clutched each other and howled. One Spoiler nicely neutralised! And then there were three. When we stopped laughing I explained to Walt about the Signs. He handled the Sea Harp, and admired the Sky Egg – he, too, could see all the wonderful swirling blues!

Our jubilation didn't last long. The phone rang, and Dad answered it.

'Catty! It's for you! Twm.'

I took the receiver from him and waited until he'd gone back into the yard. 'Hi, Twm! Oh, boy, have I got a tale to tell you!'

'Later, Catrin. I'm just outside the Toll House, down on the shore. Meet me, fast as you can.'

I hung up. Now what?

I stuck my head out the back door.

'Why did that nice Brett rush off in such a hurry?' Mom complained. 'Was it something you said to him, Catty? I think he really likes you. Did you upset him some way?'

'No idea, Mom. (Like I cared!) He just remembered something he has to do, I guess. Look, Mom, Dad, I'm just off to meet Twm, OK?'

'Will you be back for tea?'

Tea? I'd only just eaten lunch, for Pete's sake! 'Don't wait tea for me – I'll get something later if I'm hungry. See you!'

Mom set the glider swinging. I guess she was a bit disappointed that her match-making with me and Brett had ended so abruptly. Well, there wasn't a whole lot of romance in my relationship with Twm, but he was the only guy I wanted to spend time with, so she was gonna have to get used to that, right?

Twm was sitting on the pebbles beside his

upturned boat, idly shredding a piece of seaweed. I hefted my backpack with the Signs off my shoulder and sat down beside him.

'Hi. I came fast as I could. What's up?'

'Taid wants us. Now.'

'No problem. Got your fishbones?'

'Of course.' He pulled out his string, unhooked a bone, and I did the same.

I just had time to grab the Signs before the world fast-forwarded under our feet, trees, grass, sea and shore twinkling frantically past, until we gradually slowed and drifted to a stop outside Taid's cave.

I looked around me. The rocking chair moved gently in the wind of our arrival, but there was no sign of Taid. 'Where is he?'

'Inside, I suppose.'

We opened the door at the rear of the cave and went inside. Great torches illuminated the soaring ceiling, and light twinkled off the minerals and jewels speckling the walls. Taid was leaning on the great, round mirror, his beard almost touching the glass.

'About time you two got here. We've got troubles, boy.'

'What?'

'Well, to begin with, the Sea Girl has gone. I woke up this morning and her bed was empty.'

'Maybe she's gone back to her father?' I suggested, but Taid shook his head.

'No. More likely she's gone back to that Dewi. But that's not all of it.'

'What else?'

'Look.' The old man indicated the mirror.

I bent over, trying to keep the reflected light of the torches out of my eyes, but I had to search quite hard before I saw what Taid was pointing at. It was a boat, a curious looking thing with all sorts of bits sticking out all over, like diving platforms and gantries holding nets, and a bit trailing out behind, just below the surface as well. The mirror kind of zoomed in, and there in the wheelhouse beside the man at the helm was Dewi. The boat was nosing out of a port I didn't recognise.

'Where are they?'

'Not sure. I think maybe the Firth of Forth. Scotland, anyway.'

'Why Scotland, Taid?' I asked.

Twm answered. 'Because that's where the seismic oil exploration vessels come from. That's what the boat is, isn't it, Taid? They've hired it to bring down here.'

'You mean –' I stared at Twm, realisation gradually dawning.

'They're on their way to Cardigan Bay. And by the time they've finished firing off their underwater explosions, they'll not only have found the oil they're looking for, because it's almost certainly there, they'll also have driven off every seal and dolphin – and probably what's left of the bird colonies, too – between the Castlemartin Peninsula and Ynys Witrin.'

'Then we've got to stop them, Twm,' I said fiercely. 'We can still beat them, I know we can!'

CHAPTER TWENTY-ONE

'We have to stop them,' Twm said, 'but they won't be here just yet. How long do you think it will take them to get to Cardigan Bay from Scotland, Taid?'

'Depends when they left, boy. Not particularly accurate regarding time, this mirror. It's all to do with reflections bending time or something; can't say I understand the all the technicalities. But I don't reckon the Spoilers will risk showing themselves before nightfall, anyway. If the coast guard saw them, they'd be stopped straight away. Got to have permission before they do anything in the Bay that might upset the wild creatures. And they haven't got permission, that's for certain. But if they just sail in after dark and start firing off their damned explosives, well, not a lot anyone can do about it, if they aren't seen doing it.'

'Won't they be picked up on radar or something?'

Taid chuckled. 'This is Wales you're talking about, lovely girl, not NASA Ground Control!'

'Can't we do anything to stop them now?'

'Short of sinking the boat, not much,' Twm muttered. 'Wish we could do that, mind.'

'So we, like, just wait?' I asked, incredulously.

'No,' Taid put in. 'First thing, you have to find the Sea Girl. You brought her here with the fishbones, but she left under her own steam. And she isn't going to get very far on those old legs of hers. Very pretty, they are, but not a lot of use for walking. So you and Twm have to go and look for her, make sure she hasn't fallen down a mountain or something. And when you find her, see if you can talk her into going home, all right?'

'But what about the Spoilers?'

'Oh, don't you worry. I'll keep an eye on their progress in the mirror, and I'll soon get in touch with you if they show any signs of doing anything.'

Well, I guess we had our orders. Twm and I left the old man bent over the great mirror, munching on an apple and muttering to himself. He was looking a hundred per cent better since getting out of that hospital! We helped ourselves to a couple more packets of magic dust, and I checked my pocket to make sure we still had the fish-bones. We left the Signs behind for safe keeping, and set off to look for the Sea Girl.

'If we had Walt,' I said, when my feet were getting hot and tired and I was getting fed up tripping over boulders and slithering down steep mountainsides, 'Walt would be able to track her by her invisible footprints, being Native American and all.'

'Yes, but Walt isn't here,' Twm pointed out. 'So we've just got to keep looking, and unfortunately doing it on foot. She can't have got far.'

'She's gotten far enough as far as I'm concerned,' I muttered. Then I had an idea. 'Twm, maybe we *can* get Walt on the job!'

Twm stood up and shaded his eyes. 'Nope. Can't

see him anywhere around, Catrin. Wishful thinking, sorry.'

'Listen, Twm, there's a whole lot you don't know about Walt.' I quickly filled him in on the business of Walt changing to an owl and putting Dewi and Mordreda into a ditch. 'So if I use a fish-bone and go back and get him, maybe he can help us after all.'

'It's an idea.' Twm looked at his watch. 'Time's getting on. We have to find her before nightfall, in case the Spoilers make it back to Cardigan Bay tonight. It's my bet if they arrive before nightfall they'll hang back outside the Bay so they won't be spotted. I don't think they'll be back before tomorrow, but you never know. Like Taid said, the mirror isn't too accurate with time.'

'Wait here,' I ordered. I popped a fish-bone, screwed up my eyes, and thought of the apple tree in the back yard. In an instant I was there. Mom and Dad were inside the house, but Walt was sprawled in the glider, swaying gently, Madoc beside him, both fast asleep.

'Walt!' I whispered. 'Wake up!'

'Wha'?' he sat up, groggily, rubbing his eyes. 'Oh, you're back.' He yawned. 'Your Mom's a great cook, but she doesn't seem to know when to stop feeding a person.'

'You can say that again,' I agreed. 'Look, we need you. Stuff is happening. The Sea Girl has gone missing, and we need you to help us find her.'

Now he was wide awake. 'Where did she go?'

I shrugged. 'She's lost someplace in the mountains,

Taid says. But I thought, if you could come be a bird, you could help us find her. I know we could bird it, but you're better at it. You've had more practice. I'm just a bird shape. I'm still me, inside. While you –'

Walt grinned. 'I know – I can think bird, right?'

'Right!'

'Shall I shift now?'

'No. We'll use the bones to get us to Twm. You can shift when we get there.'

Walt looked kind of dubious when I handed him the fish bone, but he popped it in his mouth.

'Don't swallow it!' I warned. 'Remember to spit it out when we get back, and give it to me.'

I took his big, warm hand, and shut my eyes. When we landed at the other end, Twm was sitting on a boulder, waiting.

Walt staggered. 'Eugh. I feel real nauseous, Catty! Why didn't you warn me?'

'Sorry, forgot. Better soon, promise. Now, if you change to a bird, we'll do the same and then you can show us how to look, OK?'

Walt stretched upwards, turned slowly in a circle, and by the time he'd completed the 360° turn, a golden eagle stood in his place, its tawny crown and dark brown back unmistakable.

Twm grinned. 'If any birdwatchers see you, they'll have heart attacks. There hasn't been a golden eagle in Wales for years and years.'

Walt lifted his majestic wings and opened his hooked beak.

'And now,' I said, helping myself to a pack of fairy

191

dust from Twm's pocket, 'there are three. Like, ornithological heaven.'

'If we see any twitchers,' Twm said solemnly, 'we'll do a detour, just to make sure they see us.' And he, too, sprinkled himself.

The three of us spread our wings and took off, Walt in the lead, slightly above us, his unmistakable eagle shape making me gasp with delight, even though I knew all along it was only Walt. *Only* Walt! What was I thinking? Less than two years back, I wouldn't have believed any of this, and now, here I was, soaring over Snowdonia, wearing eagle-feathers! Like, wow!

Slithering on the down-draughts of the mountainside was like – well, the closest I can come to it is a *glissando* of feeling. Like harp music in motion. Oh, I'm not describing it too well, but it was, like, *so* fabulous. There was all this power in my wings, and the littlest twitch of the big, splayed feathers could change direction, height, all sorts of stuff. It was just amazing.

It was only minutes later that Walt spotted the little figure far below.

'Kaaaa!' he screamed, and dropped like a stone, Twm and me following. He glided in to land, and swiftly Twm and I shook ourselves free of the dust. Walt just shimmered and was Walt again.

The Sea girl – Mallt – was lying between two large rocks, asleep or unconscious. What was real weird was that her bottom half – her legs, I guess – were sort of *wavering*. One minute there would be legs there, plain as plain, the next the legs would blur and

192

a dusty, dull-looking fishtail would half-appear and then be gone.

I knelt beside her and shook her. She groaned and opened her eyes.

'Mallt? Are you OK? Did you fall?'

She shook her head, weakly. 'I must go home. My legs are too weak to carry me. Take me home, Sea-Sister? Please help me?'

I guess that was me, right? But I had to ask. 'Home, where, Mallt?'

'To my father. The old man – Myrddin, Merlin, Taid, whatever his name is in this time – says I must go back. He says that the Spoilers will take my father's kingdom and our creatures and destroy them. But first, I must tell my husband, explain why I must leave him.'

'Who, Dewi?' I could hardly believe my ears. 'You're worried about *Dewi*?'

'Of course,' she said, simply. 'He is my husband.'

'No, he isn't! Mallt, he only pretended to marry you. He's one of *them!* He's a Spoiler!'

'No!' She covered her ears with her hands. 'I don't believe you! He loves me, although I'm a fish-woman!'

'Not true, Mallt! You must believe me. It isn't true.'

She shook her head, tears pouring down her cheeks. 'If he does not love me, then I am worth nothing. How can I return to my father, failed even as a dust-walker? He will not want me.'

Walt took a hand. Twm was kind of backing off the female hysteria stuff, probably not quite knowing how to cope, not having had a whole lot to do with bawling females, I guess.

193

'Sea Girl, you don't know me. I am called He-Who-Flies-With-Eagles. Believe what Catrin tells you. She is your Sea-Sister, and I promise she speaks the truth. Dewi is a Spoiler.'

Mallt stared at him, her face tragic. Then, it hardened. 'If what you say is true, then he must be punished. Before I return, I will make him suffer for what he has done. You must help me find him!'

'He's miles away,' I blurted, 'he's on a boat in Scottish waters, on his way to Cardigan Bay. When he gets here he's gonna be exploding stuff underwater to drive off the dolphins and seals and seabirds.'

I may have imagined the flash of fury across the Sea Girl's face. Maybe I didn't.

'I shall return to my father,' she sighed. 'Please, take me to the sea. I can't walk any more.'

Her legs faded again. Walt bent and lifted her in strong arms. 'Catty, give us a couple of those fishbones, honey,' he said, opening his mouth. I unhitched two small, white discs and popped one in each mouth. 'Sea-shore, here we come,' he said.

Twm and I followed, and the three of us landed on a deserted beach inaccessible on foot. It would be just about reachable by boat, but only if the tide was right and the sea was calm. She clung to Walt's neck.

'He-who-flies-with-eagles,' she whispered. 'If I had legs, do you think you could love me?'

Walt surprised me. He bent his head and gave her a kiss. 'With legs or without, Sea Girl, you're beautiful. Yes, I could love you.'

Walt carried the Sea Girl down to the edge of the

waves, and waded out until he was waist-deep. Then he lowered her gently, the clear water sluicing dust from her tail, revealing the rainbow shimmer of the scales.

Her eyes were luminous with tears, her hair floating free around her. Suddenly, the sea was thrashing and teeming with small fish, silvery shapes bursting on the surface like iridescent bubbles, the sea thick, alive and moving with them. She swam a little way out, and the massive shoals parted to let her through. She was fluid, lithe, in her element, and all around her seals and dolphins, porpoises and the dark shapes of sharks came to escort her home. Dolphins and porpoises leapt and cavorted with joy at her return.

Then, the water calmed, and the Sea Girl was gone.

CHAPTER TWENTY-TWO

We watched until the fluid shape of the last dolphin disappeared beneath the waves, and the sun was sinking over the horizon, then we took Walt to meet Taid. I knew it was gonna be quite a meeting, but seeing the tiny old man and the great bronze Native American together was quite something.

We fish-boned back – the nauseous feeling wasn't so bad now I was getting used to travelling that way. We arrived outside the cave and it was real funny to see Walt's face when we took him inside and he saw the impossible torches burning on the walls. Impossible, because they had no fuel and yet they burned and burned and gave off a clear, unwavering light. He stood in the centre of the cave and turned, slowly.

'Wow!' he breathed, checking out the glittering walls and roof, the old wooden bed, the rocking chair, (now back inside – it looked like rain) and he hadn't spotted either Taid or the mirror yet!

Taid really should take up acting, you know! He emerged from the shadows, surrounded by a weird reddish glow (I think it was a self-generated Special Effect!), wearing his moon and stars cloak, his tall pointy hat on his head, his arms thrust into the sleeves of his robe.

Walt held his breath and stared.

Taid couldn't help it. He started to chuckle, then chortle, then guffaw, until tears ran down his face and he slapped his sides. 'Oh, your face, boy,' he said, stripping off the robe and hat and chucking them in a corner. 'Haven't bothered with that rubbish for centuries. As if anyone could wear that to work in! Stupid wide sleeves, always catching on pots and cauldrons!'

Walt grinned, sheepishly. 'You had me going there,' he admitted. 'You looked just like I always imagined a wizard would look. Come to think of it, you still look just like I imagined a wizard would look, even without the robe and hat!'

'That's because he *is* a wizard, Walt,' I chortled. 'Walt-he-who-flies-with-eagles, meet Taid – Merlin.'

The two men shook hands and assessed each other. I think they both quite liked what they saw, and the handshake lasted a real long time. Then Twm got impatient.

'We found the Sea Girl, and she's gone back to her father,' he said. 'Not before time, too. Taid, what's happened in the mirror while we were gone?' he asked, striding across the cave towards it, the rest of us following.

Taid had veiled the great, round mirror with its red cloth again, and Twm and Taid carefully uncovered it. It was blank, reflecting only the cave roof. The Sea Harp, the Sky Egg and the iron Earthstone box sat on the shiny surface near the rim.

Taid leaned on the carved wooden surround, gazing into the depths. 'Can't find any trace of that damned survey vessel,' he complained, 'so I gave up looking and went into my books, instead, researching the Signs. I knew more or less what they were and where they came from, but I confirmed why the Sky Egg is so cold, Catrin.'

'Don't tell me it's going to hatch, please Taid?'

Taid lifted the beautiful Egg. Where it had rested, ice-crystals had filmed the surface of the mirror. 'Only two things will make the Sky Egg go this cold. One, because the sea gave it shelter for centuries, it's a warning that the sea is in danger. Two, as you say, it means it's going to hatch.'

'*Hatch?*' Walt said disbelievingly. 'What into?'

'That's what eggs do, usually,' Taid said mildly. 'Hatch. And it's a dragon egg.'

'A *what?*' Walt began.

Taid told him the legend of the Sky Egg.

'You mean that's really a *dragon's egg?*' he whispered, when Taid had finished.

'The very last dragon's egg,' Taid agreed, nodding wisely.

'But you can't have a baby dragon in the twenty-first century!' Walt protested.

'Why? They had them in the first century, and the second, and a good couple of centuries before that, too.'

'All the same . . .' Walt shook his head.

'If it's any consolation,' Taid said, 'I think the reason it's so cold now is the danger to the sea, not the imminent arrival of a baby dragon.'

I took the Egg from Taid's hands and turned the

icy, smooth thing over and over, watching the swirls of gentian, azure, turquoise, sky, shadows-on-snow, bluebell, deep-sea, shift and change on its surface. Then, carefully, I put it back in its box.

Taid nodded. 'I'll tell you the Legends of the other Signs when we have time,' he promised, 'but right now, I think we ought to check on the progress of that boat!'

The four of us bent over the mirror.

'What are we supposed to see?' Walt asked, frowning into his own reflection.

'Who knows?' Taid said, wiping a smear off the glass with his shirtsleeve. 'We just need to look and be patient.'

So we looked, and were patient, but it was ages before we saw anything useful. In the end, we took it in shifts, two of us resting while the others watched, but it was nearly dawn before anything appeared in the great ring of shining glass.

Twm and Taid were resting, Walt and I looking wearily at the mirror, when suddenly it began to glow with light, bluish and intense.

'Something's happening!' I shouted, and Twm and Taid were beside us instantly.

Flashes of light arced and arrowed across the mirror, almost blinding us, and then we saw, in the mirror, the strange boat that we'd seen chugging out to sea. It wasn't chugging now. It was being tossed around on some of the most mountainous seas I'd ever set eyes upon – and certainly hoped I'd never have to sail on!

The little boat soared up to the crest of a wave the

size of a sky-scraper, and then dropped like a stone down the other side. I bent in closer, and the mirror went in for a better look. Dewi was in the wheelhouse, wearing a life-preserver, his face white with terror, clutching frantically on to the wheelsman, panicking and hindering the guy.

'Was this storm forecast, Taid?'

He peered at me over his little semi-circular spectacles. 'Can't say I get much in the way of weather forecasts up here, lovely girl. Reception's a bit difficult when a person hasn't got a television.'

'I can answer that one,' Walt said. 'No, it wasn't. I heard the shipping forecast on the radio, and there weren't any storms predicted at all. The day was supposed to be dead calm.'

'Then where's it come from?' Twm wondered.

'Ah, storms blow up from nowhere,' I said. But then, into my mind flashed the memory of the Sea Girl's expression when I'd told her where Dewi was and what he was doing. That strange look that had flashed across her face. I shivered.

'I think this is the Sea Girl's revenge,' I said, slowly. 'I think she's doing this.'

I stepped back from the mirror, back as far as I could go and still see into it. 'Look!'

The mirror image drew back, too, out and out, like a camera panning away for a long shot. There was a storm at sea, but it was *entirely concentrated on one little area.* The area that happened to contain a small boat loaded with compressed air explosive charges bound for Cardigan Bay and its wild creatures.

'She's going to drown them all!' I breathed. 'Not only Dewi who probably deserves it, but the crew on board as well. And it isn't their fault, is it? They're just doing their jobs.'

'There's nothing you can do about it!' Walt said. 'They're all gonna die, aren't they? And all because we talked the Sea Girl into going back.'

'Because I told her Dewi didn't love her, more likely,' Twm said, glumly. 'It's probably my fault.'

I watched the little boat being hurled about like a cork in a washing machine. Then, suddenly, I noticed Taid was watching me, carefully, and I remembered.

'Wait!' I blurted. 'I'm the Sea Girl, too! If she can start the storm, maybe I can make her stop it!'

'It's worth a chance, I suppose,' Twm said. 'But do we really want to save a Spoiler?'

'Of course we don't,' I said, indignantly, 'but if saving him is the price we have to pay to save the innocent people on board, then yes, we do!'

Twm sighed. 'So what are we going to do?'

'We're going swimming. Walt, stay here with Taid until we get back.'

The big man nodded. 'Good luck. I've a feeling you're gonna need it.'

'Yeah. Me, too. And to think that only a week or two back I was safe out of all this in La Rochelle, learning to speak French like a native. Well, like a native speaks English, I guess!' I said, remembering Madame's attempts. 'Well, this won't get the baby fried,' I said. 'Come on, Twm!'

'Fried baby?' Walt asked, confused.

'Just a saying. Like "get the bacon bathed", you know?' He still looked blank. 'Oh, never mind. See you guys soon.'

Twm and I stepped outside the cave and each put one of our dwindling stock of fish-bones into our mouths.

The rising sun threw long, sinister shadows of the cliffs across the silky sand. Twm and I stripped off (I was getting used to swimming in my underwear these days) and hurled ourselves into the sea. We swam out as far as we could, and offshore the dolphins were waiting. We grasped a flipper each, and hung on while we were towed far out to sea, out beyond the shadowy underwater tower-shapes of Cantre'r Gwaelod, far out, where, if we'd been on the surface, the coast of Wales would have disappeared entirely into the morning haze.

The lemony morning sun reached us out here, dappling our bodies and the smooth grey shapes of the chirping, clicking dolphins leaping high out of the water and arrowing down, with scarcely a splash, for the joy of it. Oh, I wanted them to be safe – and they were going to be, if it was up to me!

Eventually, the dolphins slowed and stopped, we released the two that were towing us, and each creature gently bumped noses with us, as if it were wishing us luck, or maybe thanking us. And then they were gone.

I turned, slowly, in the water, looking around me.

A little way off, there were sharks . . .

CHAPTER TWENTY-THREE

Yeah, I know Twm said they weren't the sort of sharks that chew people. But they've still got teeth, right? And even if they bite by mistake, it's still a bite, isn't it? And maybe they don't *know* they aren't supposed to bite!

To my complete horror, Twm *swam towards them!* I had to follow, because I saw that the sinister pack of missile shapes had divided and now they were all round us, silent and scary. Oh, I so wanted to be elsewhere!

When we reached the biggest shark, it nosed Twm, and with a flick of its tail, set off into the deep, mysterious blue ahead of us. Twm reached for my hand and held it tight. Maybe he knew I was thinking of taking off! The sharks fell into formation around us, hemming us in, forcing us onward into deep water.

'Twm?' I squeaked.

'What?'

'They're herding us!'

'Escorting us, Catrin.'

'It feels more like herding to me. Where do you think we're going?'

'At a rough guess, to the Sea Girl. Or maybe her father.'

'The Sea King? They're leading us to him, do you think?'

Twm's look was kind of exasperated. 'Looks like it.'

The sharks drew us on and on, deeper and deeper, to where the only light came from a peculiar phosphorescent glow that clung to their circling bodies.

Finally we reached the Sea King's domain. Great arches and towers of coral soared over us, strange undersea creatures flocked round us, and I had the weirdest sensation that every step – stroke? – of the way, we were being watched. The sharks nudged us onward, and at last we came to a low archway that was screened by floating curtains of weed. Twm held the hanging stuff aside, and I swam through. The sharks flicked their tails and swam a little way off, their flat eyes watching, waiting . . .

Inside the curtain there was light: luminous fish and plants gave everything an eerie glow, and a large mirror, the twin of the one in Taid's cave, hung on the wall. In its depths I could make out the survey ship, tossing and rolling sickeningly on the turbulent sea.

The Sea Girl was lying on a bed that seemed to be made of the bones of some huge creature: a triangular skull the size of an elephant's decorated the bed-head, and giant ribs curved up and around it. Everywhere were chests and boxes, some open, displaying jewelled cups and plates, golden coins and rings, necklaces and brooches of every description, gleaming in the underwater light. The Sea Girl's strange, green eyes flicked over us, and then she looked away.

'What do you want?' she asked, draping a rope of pearls around her wrist. The creamy beads slithered down her greenish-white arm. 'Why have you come?'

'Sea Girl,' Twm said sternly, 'if it's you that's making the storm, trying to sink the Spoilers' ship, you have to stop it. It isn't right.'

'What?' She sat up, suddenly, her eyes narrowed. She was different, here, from the way she'd been on land. There, she'd been a helpless, pitiable creature, unsure of where she belonged, pining for both a man who didn't want her, didn't really love her, and longing for her undersea home. Here, she was imperious and powerful, frighteningly cold. 'I don't *have* to do anything. I am the Sea King's Daughter. I shall do what I wish to do.'

'Even when what you wish is wrong?' Twm asked, mildly.

'Wrong? *Wrong?* How dare you suggest that anything I do is wrong!' she hissed angrily. 'My father destroyed Cantre'r Gwaelod and all its people. I can certainly destroy one little, insignificant ship. I have a right. The people on it are all Spoilers. They mean to harm Our Kingdom. They deserve to die. And die they shall.'

'Only one of the people on board that boat is a Spoiler, Mallt. The others are innocent. They don't know what the Spoilers plan to do.'

'That doesn't make them innocent. They know what their boat does, they know that the machines they carry will drive off the birds, the dolphins and porpoises – even the fish will go if these people are

205

allowed to live. They are just as guilty as the Spoilers.'

'If you sink that boat, Sea Girl, you will be as bad as any Spoiler. They see only what they want, and allow nothing to stand in their way. Isn't that what you're doing?' Twm's face was white and drawn.

'Why are you pleading for them? I thought that you and my Sea-Sister were against these Spoilers. Let them die. They deserve it.'

'We are against the Spoilers all the way, sure we are,' I put in, 'but they aren't all Spoilers on that boat. We're asking you to spare them, Mallt.'

'No. He must die.'

I was on that in a flash. 'He? Oh, you mean Dewi, I suppose. So it isn't about the prospecting ship at all, then. It's just about your hurt feelings, is it? You're willing to let everyone on that ship die, just to get your own back on Dewi? That's not fair, Sea Girl.'

'Fair? You think I care what is fair? I would drown your whole wretched country to revenge myself on him. He hurt me. He called me fish-woman. Just like the other one. He deserves to die.'

I got kind of exasperated at all these Teen Queen shenanigans. 'Oh, for goodness sake, Mallt! D'you think no one's ever been dumped before? Get a life! Get over it. We all get dumped once or twice in our lives. It's part of growing up. I've been dumped loads of times, and I survived! My Mom would say there's more fish in the sea than ever came out of it. Find someone else!'

Twm raised his eyebrows. 'More fish in the sea?

206

Well, I suppose that's appropriate, Catrin! Maybe not too tactful, but appropriate.'

I scowled at him, too. 'I mean, take Twm for instance. You don't see me, like, drowning people just because he hasn't –' I suddenly realised what I was saying, and clamped my mouth shut, fast. Even underwater I felt myself start blushing.

Twm glanced at me, startled, but didn't say anything, thank goodness. Well OK, so I really, really like Twm. So what?

The Sea Girl narrowed her eyes and stared at me. 'So what should I do? Marry a *fish-man*? Never! I am the Sea King's Daughter!'

'So what? You're half fish, aren't you? So's your Dad, although I haven't had the pleasure of meeting him. What's wrong with that? Nothing to be ashamed of. You got a tail, I got legs. You live under the sea, I live on land. Horses for courses, yeah?' Even Twm was looking kinda confused, but I knew what I meant.

'What I'm saying, Mallt, is that you've gotten mad because that dumb Dewi called you a fish-woman. But you *are* half fish, half girl, and now you're turning up your nose at perfectly nice guys just because *they've* got tails! It doesn't make sense, does it? Look, basically, everyone's equal, whether they're half fish, all fish, or whatever, right? So get a life, Sea Girl!'

Her eyebrows were drawn together in a scowl. 'How dare you –' she began, 'how dare you say we are equal! I am the Sea Girl!'

'And so am I, you utter dork!' I shrieked back,

207

'and you aren't listening to me. Stop that storm, rescue those poor guys on the boat, or else.'

'Or else what? You're threatening me? If you're the Sea Girl, then *you do it*!'

We suddenly all went very quiet and stared at each other. Twm was staring at me.

I took a deep breath – even though I was underwater, it didn't matter – and decided. 'All right, I will. I'll stop the storm. But it's really time you grew up, you know, and stopped feeling sorry for yourself.'

And on that passing shot I put my nose in the air and swam out the sea-weedy doorway to where the sharks waited. That slowed me up some, but not entirely. Twm tapped me on the shoulder.

'Excuse me, Catrin?'

'What?'

'Do you really think you can do it? Stop the storm, I mean.'

'How do I know?'

'But you said –'

'I *know* what I *said*, Twm, OK? And there must be some way of stopping it, right. If she can start a storm, then maybe I can stop it.'

'Oh, great,' Twm said. 'What are you going to do, ask it nicely?'

'Smart-ass!' I said, crossly. 'No, I'm gonna concentrate real hard and see if that does it. But first, I've got to find that darn ship.'

I fumbled in my pocket, found one of the few remaining fishbones, popped it in my mouth. I didn't know if it would work underwater, but it seemed to be worth the risk, I guess. Actually, thinking about it, it could have been real nasty: I could have gotten the bends, or imploded or something like that, but I just ended up bobbing around in the raging sea surrounding the oil-survey boat.

What made it all the more annoying was that half a mile away the sky was blue and the sea flat calm. It was just inside the threatening circle of the Sea King's Daughter's magical storm that things were kinda hairy! I let myself sink below the waves. It was still rough down there, but not as bad as it was getting chucked about on the surface. I didn't really know where to begin, to stop a storm. I mean, OK, I'm the Sea Girl too, but I didn't have a whole lot of experience of storm-stopping – or starting, for that matter. None at all, in fact. I shut my eyes and tried to concentrate despite the rolling and pitching of the sea around me.

And then, into my head came Taid's voice.

'That's it, Catrin, just think it calm. Ignore the storm, it isn't real. *Think* it calm. Imagine a –'

His voice was gone. Imagine? Imagine what, for Pete's sake?

Then, quite suddenly, a tremendous feeling of peace came over me. I stopped panicking, and I started thinking calm thoughts. Smooth sand, glassy, wet and barred like a mackerel where the tide had been. White gulls wheeling over calm blue seas. Tiny little inoffensive wavelings tiptoeing up onto the shore, little foamy lacy bits hissing as they sank into the sand. No waves, no whitecaps, no swell, just flat – calm – blue – peaceful – gentle – mill-pond – sea.

I rose slowly to the surface, and my head broke through into sunshine. It had stopped raining, and although there was still something of a swell, the angry roaring, the lashing winds and pounding rain were quickly dying away. A little way off, the survey boat gave a half-turn, then set its rudder into the sea and began to get underway again.

The sea became as innocuous as a bathtub. I had done it. I had calmed the storm.

But now the boat was heading, with its cargo of compressed air explosive charges all ready to fire off in the very places where the dolphins, the seals, the sea-birds and the fish thought they were safe.

I groaned. We were back where we started. Had I done the wrong thing? Maybe I should just have let the boat sink.

CHAPTER TWENTY-FOUR

The sea was flat calm, and the boat was now determinedly heading for the deep waters of Cardigan Bay. Suddenly, Twm was beside me in the water, his face alight with happiness and relief.

'You did it! You stopped the storm!'

'Yeah, sure,' I said disconsolately. 'And now there's nothing to stop the survey boat from firing off its depth charges and driving the dolphins away – or worse. We've lost, Twm, and all because we couldn't sacrifice one boatload of blokes to save the whole Bay and all its creatures.'

'We haven't lost yet. There must be a way to stop them. They won't do anything until it's dark, so we've got a couple of hours. And we've still got the Signs.'

'Yeah, right.' I began swimming towards the shore. 'And it's gonna take us most of the couple of hours to get home. I'm fresh out of fishbones, Twm, and I'm so tired. At least I can't drown.'

'Here,' Twm trod water, fumbling in his pocket. 'Have one of mine. These are my last two, but they'll get us back to Taid.'

They did. We were outside the cave in a flash, and too late I remembered that our clothes were on the beach. Oh, great. Me in my underwear, Mom was gonna be real ecstatic, right?

But Taid had thought of that, and somehow had

retrieved them for us. Walt had returned to the Toll House already, but our clothes were in a neat pile. Shivering and goose-bumpy, I tugged on my levis and t-shirt, and slumped on the bed. Taid sat in his rocking chair, tipping himself gently back-and-forth with his toes, watching us.

'Well done, Catrin. You saved those seamen. It was the right thing to do.'

'Was it? I'm not convinced, Taid. Now they will just go ahead and wreck the Bay anyway, and we'll have failed.'

'Oh, come on, lovely girl! You've still got the Signs, haven't you? There must be something you can do.'

I shook my head, sadly. I was so darn tired I couldn't think straight. 'I don't think so. The only Spoiler we've neutralised successfully is Brett, and I sent him off to join –'

I looked at Twm. He stared back at me.

'– the Save our Seashores Society!' I crowed. 'That's it! Taid, we're both out of fishbones. Do you have any more? And we need a telephone directory –'

'No we don't. The group meets in Aberystwyth. I belong to it. Someone has to keep an eye on what they do.'

Taid had already reached into thin air and produced a phone book. He threw it upwards and it disappeared again. 'Have you got the old fishbones?'

I took the string of blackened bones out of my pocket and handed it over. Twm did the same. Taid took them, opened a stone jar, and dropped the two sets inside. He gave the jar a vigorous shake, like he was making a cocktail or something, opened it and tipped out two strings of newly whitened bones onto the mirror. Powder drifted and clouded, and Twm blew it away.

'Take the Signs, and go, quickly now,' Taid ordered. 'It will soon be dark enough for them to start firing off depth charges, so there's no time to lose.'

I fumbled the still-icy Sky Egg and the Sea Harp into my backpack, and Twm settled the Earthstone's box into his. We both slipped a fishbone onto our tongues, held hands (I didn't know where we were going, but holding hands felt good anyway) and in the twinkle of a star, we were standing in an Aberystwyth back street full of terraced Victorian houses.

Twm looked around him. 'It's number 47 – there it is.' He hared across the road, me galloping behind, the backpack bouncing between my shoulder blades. 'Let me do the talking this time, all right?' he said. 'I know them. They're all surf-bums, but they're well-meaning enough blokes. But get ready with the Sky Egg when I play the Sea Harp. Got it?'

'Yeah, got it,' I panted, charging up the marble steps behind him. I unslung my pack and passed him the Harp. The Sky Egg was covered in a thin film of clear ice, and the blue swirling patterns seemed sluggish and dulled. I put it to my ear. I thought I could hear a faint tapping, but – nah. Must be my imagination. A dragon hatchling running around in Aberystwyth, 2004? Like, no way!

In answer to Twm's knock, footsteps thumped

towards the door, which opened to reveal a suspicious-looking, bespectacled boy, in baggy surfer shorts and bare feet, his tatty hair salt-blonde.

'What?' he asked truculently.

'Hello, Huw. It's me, Twm.'

'Hey, dude! I can see that. What do you want? Haven't got a SOSS meeting tonight. Next Monday, dude, cool with you?' And he began to close the door.

Twm's foot shot out and blocked it. His hands fluttered across the strings of the Sea Harp, and the boy froze, his shoulders slumped, his mouth half open. I clutched the Sky Egg and started talking.

'No, you're wrong. You need to call a meeting right now, urgently. Start phoning. Get everybody you can round here. Tell them it's an emergency.'

'Especially Ianto,' Twm added. 'Tell him to bring his boat round to the sea front. We're going to need it.' Twm twanged the strings again, and the boy twitched and blinked.

'Oh, yeah, hi Twm. Come on in. I'll get on the blower to the lads, get 'em round. Dunno why they're late, 'specially with a real bad 'mergency. You use the phone, dude, I'll use my mobile. There's a list of numbers there.'

It didn't take long to round up the SOSS members, including Ianto and his boat, and – to my amusement – an earnest-looking Brett now out of his smart chinos and into surfer baggies. Obviously my instruction to the Spoiler to join something environmental and do good works had hit home! When they were all gathered – mostly student surfer types, from the look

214

of them, one or two slightly beery from the Union bar up on the hill – Twm tinkled the Harp.

I clutched the Sky Egg, and told our unlikely looking sea-saviours what was going to happen.

'There's an oil-survey boat,' I explained. 'It's standing off Cardigan Bay waiting for nightfall. When no one can see them, they are going to sail into the Bay and set off underwater air charges. The way it works is, sound echoes off the deposits of oil under the sea-bed, and that's how they know it's there. But the noise and shock-waves of the explosions will drive the dolphins away, and the porpoises, and disturb the birds. And if they do discover oil, there's gonna be pollution as well, guys. We gotta do something, or it's surfing in a sea of dead creatures, right?'

They couldn't reply, of course, being frozen by the Sea Harp, but I could tell from their eyes that they understood.

'So what we're going to do,' Twm said, taking the Sky Egg from me, 'is get on Ianto's boat, go out and stop them. Understood?'

They sat absolutely still. I suddenly remembered, and played the Harp again. They went into action straight away. Twm and I put down the Signs and struggled into flotation-jackets someone found for us – not that we needed them, but it seemed easier to put them on than argue. In a matter of minutes we were all kitted up and heading for the sea-front, where Ianto's boat was hauled up onto the pebbles. The sun was almost gone now, sitting like half a red tennis ball on the horizon. We carried the boat out until it floated, then all piled on board, and Ianto fired up the outboard. A bearded student in denim cut-offs unfurled a large Save Our Seas Society banner that flapped in the wind as we bounced across the darkening sea.

The survey boat was gradually slithering into the Bay with the coming of night, and on deck men were running about checking equipment and getting ready to lower the explosive devices. As soon as we spotted them, Ianto, his face set in a fearsome scowl, hit the gas and the boat's speed increased until we were kind of doing the boat equivalent of a bike-wheelie! We shot across the bows of the survey vessel, waving our flag and shouting. Whoever was on watch either ignored us or didn't see us, and the boat kept going. Then, one or two of the seamen noticed, word was passed to the bridge, and gradually the boat slowed and stopped.

We pulled alongside. A row of heads looked down on us from a great height.

'What do you want?' a surly voice bellowed.

Brett shouted back, 'To talk to Dewi,'

'Dewi? Couldn't you have phoned?'

'Ha, ha. Very funny. Could you get him, please?'

Seconds later Dewi's face peered down at us. 'Brett? What you doing there? We looked for you everywhere! Should have been on this trip, boy. Let me down, you did.'

Brett put on a sort of heroic face. 'I would have let myself down if I'd joined you. What you are doing is wrong. You don't have any right to do this to the Bay. Think about the wildlife, Dewi! Turn this boat round and go back to where you came from.'

Dewi scowled. 'What's got into you? I thought you were one of us.'

'Not any longer. Now I'm on the side of the sea, and if you don't turn back, well . . .' Brett glared upwards.

'Well, what?' Dewi asked.

Brett sat down, suddenly. He didn't know, 'well, what?'

Neither did I. One of the ship's crew stared down at us. 'You're wrong, laddie, to think we've no permission to survey,' he said, in a broad Scottish accent. 'We've a permit, right enough. Dewi told us that all the papers were in order, else we'd not have put to sea in the first place.'

Dewi put on a serious face. 'Oh, yeah. Right. Permit, yeah, all in order. Trust me.'

'So you say,' Twm shouted angrily. 'But has anyone ever seen it?'

The crew looked from one to the other, shaking their heads. 'When they hired us and the vessel, they told us they had permission,' the Scot said, frowning.

'And you believed them?' Twm bellowed. 'Without seeing the proof?'

The Scottish seaman shrugged. 'Well, yes. Why would we not believe the man?'

I tugged Twm's sleeve. 'Twm, I don't know why we're arguing with them. We've still got the Signs, haven't we? We can –'

Except we hadn't, had we. I suddenly remembered putting them down to put on the flotation jacket. I didn't remember picking them up again. We'd left them behind. We stared at each other, horrified. The magical Signs that would have gotten us right out of this mess, and stopped the ship going any further into the Bay, and certainly stopped them firing off their explosives, were sitting on a coffee table in scruffy student accommodation in downtown Aberystwyth.

'Oh, *shoot*!' I moaned. 'What now?'

Twm clutched the sides of the bobbing boat and looked defeated. 'We could go back and get them, I suppose,' he suggested.

'And they're gonna sit here and wait for us? Sure they are. And when we get back with the Signs, the Spoiler is either gonna sink this little boat and make us lose the Signs, or he's gonna get us on board and steal them from us. There must be some other way –'

I stared at the black-painted sides of the boat rising above us. A short time before, they had been battered by pounding seas, and now they floated, barely moving, in calm water. Fiercely, I wished I'd let them sink.

CHAPTER TWENTY-FIVE

Then, inspiration struck. I leaned forward and whispered in Twm's ear.

At first, he stared at me, but when he thought about it, a slow grin spread across his face. He shed his life-jacket, stood up in the little boat, stripped off (yet again) and slipped over the side into the calm water. No way was I stripping off in front of all those guys, so I just took off my flotation jacket and dived in. The SoSS students watched us open-mouthed, and so did the sailors on the survey vessel.

We didn't care about revealing secrets: this was an emergency. We swam down and down, and Twm began to call the dolphins – although they had been warned against answering to their Seanames, they recognised Twm's voice and trusted him enough to obey. The weird, unearthly pinging, squeaking and clicking spread out underwater, bounced from dolphin to dolphin. Then he began on the porpoises, and one by one, in families and pods, they came to us. They swam around us, a mass of lithe, moving creatures, and then the seals came: common seals, one or two grey seals that had strayed into the Bay, with their longer muzzles and flatter heads, intelligent, dog-like faces watching us, inquisitive whiskers bristling. Fish came in their millions: cod and mackerel, dogfish, all the common fish, and even some of the blind, pale deep-sea varieties, all of them came to Twm's call. Sharks came, and even a Minke whale strayed from the north came to investigate what was going on, its mild, friendly eye and massive body gliding past me like a long grey dream of pure delight.

When they were all assembled, Twm and I swam upward to the surface, and heaved ourselves back into the boat. I was shivering, but it was with excitement, not cold. The light was gone, now, just a sunglow on the horizon remaining, and the survey vessel bobbed on a dark sea, red and green riding lights twinkling.

I stood up in the little boat and called up to the crew. 'Hey, you guys! Do you want to see what is going to suffer if you go ahead with the survey? Look!'

Twm slapped his hand on the water, three times.

At once, the sea began to churn and boil. Dorsal shark fins sliced through the waves; dolphins leapt upwards; porpoises danced around the boats. Seals stuck their intelligent heads out of the water and stared, their liquid eyes accusing. There were shouts from on board the ship, and suddenly searchlights came on, playing across the dark water, illuminating the churning, throbbing, boiling mass of sea creatures.

The SOSS guys in our boat were totally wiped out, I mean, like, majorly overcome. Huw was actually crying with joy, and the others weren't far off. Most people count themselves lucky if they see a single dolphin in their whole life, and here was the entire population of the Bay. The great grey-blue creatures nudged the little boat with their bottle-noses, squeaked, and allowed themselves to be patted and kissed. Three or four of the surfer guys slipped over the side and into the water with them. The vast grey back of the whale surfaced a little way off, and water gushed from its blowhole, startling everybody with the sudden noise, and then its mighty flukes rose dripping from the sea before it dived again, slapping down and splattering us all with cold water.

Then Twm sent out an order that was heard by the nearest dolphins, and passed on. One by one the creatures sank into the depths and departed, until all that was left was a solitary grey seal, watching us solemnly, and then the dark head sank beneath the sea and was gone.

'Oh, wow!' Huw breathed, wiping his eyes and nose on his T-shirt sleeve. 'Oh, man, that was so coool!' His smile was pure happiness, and Brett was like, totally speechless.

They all looked at each other. 'No one's ever going to believe us when we tell them,' Ianto said, snuffling happily.

Twm and I exchanged glances and grinned at each other. When we got back to Aberystwyth we'd make sure they'd never tell anybody. We had the Signs, right? The question was, would our plan work?

'Hey, you aboard the survey boat?'

The row of heads appeared again, back-lit by the searchlights. I couldn't make out which one was Dewi's.

'How did you do that?' the Scottish voice said in the darkness.

'Doesn't matter,' Twm said. 'Thing is, what are you going to do? Are you going to go ahead and explode those things, knowing that all those creatures are going to suffer because of it? Or are you going to do the right thing and go back to Scotland? Because I can tell you there's no permission to survey. The Spoiler – Dewi, I mean – is lying if he says there is.'

One of the heads withdrew, and the Scottish accent said, 'Is that true, young Dewi?'

'True? Of course it's not!' he shouted angrily. 'Are you going to believe a scruffy lot of beach bums? Who's paying you? Me, right? And I'm paying you to find oil under the Bay, so get on with it!'

'Show us the permit, Dewi.'

'I've, I've – forgotten to bring it. But it's there, back in the office.'

'Och, I'm sure it is,' the Scot said mockingly, 'but you'll pardon me, laddie, if under the circumstances I do not believe you until I see it?'

'It's there, it's there!' Dewi screamed.

'Aye, it may well be, but after what I've seen tonight, I don't intend to do anything but turn this boat around and head home.'

'You won't get a penny of what I promised you unless you do the survey!' Dewi threatened angrily.

'Oh, but we shall, my little man,' the Scot said silkily, 'for did you not read the contract you signed? Our pay started the minute the engines did, survey or not, and the longer we hang about here, the more it will cost you.'

'I don't believe this!' Dewi screamed. 'You can't

turn back! The Spoilers will –'   We didn't get to hear what the Spoilers would do, because the sound of the survey vessel's engines turning over drowned it out.

Back on dry land we let the surfer guys high-five and "hey-dude" all the way back to Huw's place, and have an hour or two sinking cans of beer and raving about the dolphins and porpoises, and 'oh, hey, wow, dude, man, the whale, remember the whale?' Then we zapped them with the Sea Harp and the Sky Egg, and hey, dude, wow, they forgot the whole thing. OK, maybe it was kinda cruel to do that to them after they'd helped us, but we couldn't risk our secret appearing on *Wales Today* or in *The Western Mail,* could we? And the way they were talking, it would have. The guys on the survey vessel, well we had to gamble that they'd keep quiet about it – especially since what they'd been about to do had been illegal.

Twm and I collected our Signs (and this time, we hadn't even had to use the Earthstone) and left, heading back to the cave and Taid. We reported our victory, and Taid smiled with satisfaction.

'Knew you'd do it,' he said smugly. 'So did Walt. Said he had a feeling. I like that young man. He's one of us, you know.'

'Yeah, I know,' I said. 'Walt's way cool. I'll be sorry to see him go back to the States.'

'He'll go,' Taid said, 'but he'll come back.' He smiled, mysteriously. 'He's got himself a bit attached to the place, somehow. All to do with ancestry, and blood, and probably Prince Madoc being in there somewhere. We'll be seeing him again, don't you worry. Now,' he went on, 'tell me. You beat the Spoilers?'

'Yeah. It was kinda hairy out there for a while, Taid,' I said, 'and I thought we'd blown it at one stage, but thanks to Twm, we won this time. Oh, wow, you should have seen all those dolphins, and seals, and porpoises, and there was even a whale! They helped us beat them.'

'This time. Yes,' Taid said, adding thoughtfully, 'I've been thinking about those Signs, lovely girl.'

'What about them, Taid,' Twm asked, frowning. 'I suppose we should give them back. They ought to stay with her.'

'Oh, I think they should stay with the Sea Girl, all right,' Taid agreed. 'But the Sea Girl is standing right beside you, Twm. And it's my belief that the Signs would be safer with Catrin than with Mallt. No more sense than a winkle, that one. Catrin is far more sensible. She doesn't go getting all silly and hysterical about the first lad she meets to bat her eyelashes at, does she?'

'Thing is, Taid,' I said, trying real hard not to bat mine at Twm, 'those Signs are real scary.'

'Oh, yes indeed they are,' the old man agreed, stroking his beard. 'But if the Spoilers come again – or rather, *when* they do, because they will not be beaten for long – do you want to have to go chasing after that flibbertigibbet to get them back?'

Twm and I exchanged glances. 'No!' Twm said. '*Dim diolch, Taid!*'

I wasn't quite so confident. 'Taid?'

He looked up at me, twinkling blue eyes. 'Mmhm?'

'If we decide not to give the Signs back to the Sea King's Daughter, will you keep them for me? Take care of them, maybe leave them up here where they'll be safe when you decide to go back to the cottage? Then we could get at them if we need them, right?'

'I don't see why not. They'll be safe enough. A Spoiler won't venture into this place. And they'd still be yours, the Sea Girl's, so The Legend would be satisfied.'

'Especially the Sky Egg,' I said, sighing with relief. 'Boy, what'd I do if it hatched?'

'Have you looked at it since you got back?'

I shook my head, opened the box and lifted out my beautiful blue Egg.

It was smooth, slippery – and warm. I guess I didn't have to worry about baby-sitting a dragon just yet! All the same, I was kind of disappointed in a weird way. A baby dragon would have been real neat!

Twm decided to stay in the cave and look after Taid a while, especially since Cei was still with Rhodri. Taid was much better, but he was still looking frail and old. Yeah, I know he's a couple of centuries ancient and magic, too, but he still needed taking care of, OK?

'I guess I'd better get back to the Toll House. Mom's probably forgotten what I look like – I've hardly been there since I got back from France. Still, with any luck she'll be so wrapped up in her bear-making that she won't have missed me too much.'

'If you get into trouble because of it, we can always zap her and your Dad with the Harp and the Egg, I suppose,' Twm suggested, grinning. 'Nothing like a bit of magic to make people forgetful.'

'Yeah, we could. But hey, what can she do, ground me until I put down roots and grow little green apples?'

'Yes, probably.'

'All the same, whatever happens, I'll ride it out. Hey, Twm, we did it! We trashed the Spoilers again!'

'Yes. This time we did. But don't forget – three of them are still out there, Catrin. Don't ever forget that. And sooner or later, they'll find a fourth, and then they'll be strong again.'

'I guess. But meanwhile – life goes on, right?'

'Right.' He stood next to me in the moonlight, his hands shoved deep in his jeans pocket, staring at his feet. 'Catrin?'

'Yeah?'

'Do you think your Mam and Dad will send you off somewhere else?'

'What, to learn Chinese in Peking or Russian in Vladivostok, you mean?'

'Somewhere. Get you away from me again, wouldn't it?'

I grinned up at him. 'Hey, Twm?'

'Yes?'

'They can send me to the moon if they like. But I don't think they will. And if they do – I'll run away and come back here. Because no way – no, no, no way, Twm, read my lips – am I leaving you, or Wales again!'

'In that order, Catrin?'

'In that order, Twm.'

I guess now you'd really like to know if he kissed me, right?

Well, guys, that's for me to know and you to find out, right?

Right.

AUTHOR'S END NOTE

Those fans of the earlier book in this series, *The Back End of Nowhere,* whom I've met and spoken to in schools, libraries and bookshops over the years, may know that on the day I finished the first draft, the oil tanker *Sea Empress* hit the rocks at Milford Haven. The disaster that the Three Signs averted in the book actually happened in real life.

Sad to report, on the day I finished *Nowhere Again* in first draft, the news appeared in *The Western Mail* that the first cases of PDV (Phocine [seal] Distemper Virus) were detected in the seal population of East Anglia. The last epidemic of this virus in 1988-89 caused the deaths of up to 19,000 common seals and 300-400 grey seals in European waters, and this outbreak has already killed more than 2000 seals in Scandinavia.

Although in the book I have Catrin and Twm helping to immunise the seals against the virus, unfortunately there is as yet no vaccine that can cure the disease, which is spread by coughing and sneezing when the seals are beached.

I am indebted to Rod Penrose, Strandings Co-ordinator (Wales), based at Llechryd in Cardigan, for help and information.